Cleve

Clevenger Gold

The True Story of Murder and Unfound Treasure*

S. E. Swapp

*An estimated $1 million worth, still buried, we believe, in a pot in the Buckskin Mountains!

Edited by David Aretha

gatekeeper press

Published by Gatekeeper Press
3971 Hoover Rd. Suite 77
Columbus, OH 43123-2839

Layout Design by: Mr. Merwin D. Loquias

eISBN: 9781619845442
Paperback: 9781619845473
Hardcover: 9781619845480

Printed in the United States of America

Contents

Preface 7

Intro *Unfound Treasure* 9

Chapter 1 *August 8, 1887 Prescott Prison, Arizona Territory* 11

Chapter 2 *February 6, 1886* 15

Chapter 3 *August 1887 Prescott Prison, Arizona Territory—Cold Fate* 27

Chapter 4 *February 18, 1886 Parral, Chihuahua, Mexico* 29

Chapter 5 *February 20, 1886 Graham County, Arizona Territory* 39

Chapter 6 *March 20, 1886 Holbrook, Arizona Territory* 45

Chapter 7 *April 10, 1886 Near Willow Springs Fort, Arizona Territory* 51

Chapter 8 *A Bit Friendly* 61

Chapter 9 *May 5, 1886 Lee's Ferry, Grand Canyon, Arizona Territory* ...65

Chapter 10 *May 16-19, 1886 Jacob's Pool to House Rock Springs* 79

Chapter 11 *May 20, 1886 Buckskin Mountain* 85

Chapter 12 *May 22, 1886 Kanab, Utah Territory* 99

Chapter 13 *Toquerville, Utah Territory* 105

Chapter 14 *Coyotes and Cadavers* 109

Chapter 15 *A Sheriff's Hunt October 31, 1886* 113

Chapter 16 *Reckoning* 117

Chapter 17 *August 7, 1887 Prescott, Arizona Territory Prison* 127

Chapter 18 *August 11, 1887 Shave & uh Haircut* 135

END *March 2003 Utah/Arizona Border* 139

Preface

$\mathcal{T}$his is the true story of the Clevenger family from Arizona Territory, and their unfortunate events as they trekked north to Washington Territory. Once the old, cantankerous Sam Clevenger and his wife, Charlotte, hired Frank Willson and John Johnson to help with the move, their fate took a dark turn. These true events were documented by journalists through the 1887 trial and well into the 1900s, and stories have been told of Sam's unfound treasure for nearly 130 years. But, this is the first detailed, documented, and vetted account of their bizarre and fascinating tale.

Intro

Unfound Treasure

*A*lthough it is not the point or the main focus of this story, it is definitely quite interesting. There is a treasure in the Northern Arizona Buckskin Mountains that has yet to be found—a treasure potentially worth a million bucks.

For real.

I have nearly pinpointed this treasure thanks largely to the handwritten documentation I have compiled from county, state, territorial, and national archives. Documented occurrences with specific timelines are period accurate based on a Yavapai County, Arizona Territory, court case involving individuals with their own testimony as stated in an actual murder trial.

History can be easily skewed by translations of the media, word of mouth, and human nature. As newspapers and reporters delivered this story slowly east for years after the incidents (as far as New York City), the story was so mistranslated that a half-black man became a white man, and even the last names of the individuals were swapped in certain cases, further confusing the truth. Treasure magazines, newspaper articles, and local gurus have relied upon stories that altered locations, dates, and individuals involved with no supporting evidence. In some cases these alterations appeared to be concealing the evidence of the treasure location, possibly with some purpose or merely by accident.

Although this story is written as historical fiction, the basic facts herein are absolutely accurate to the timeline and locations. I say this within the certainty of 1886 records handwritten by the actual parties involved. Confessions and lies are exposed to the nth detail, not to be confused with hearsay from years of different stories being bent from ear to ear.

A U.S. Cavalry Colt Single Action Army pistol, with a U,S. marked, matched serial number, was found in the newly mapped areas. Recent and detailed research uncovered other period-correct artifacts that matched the timelines. The modern technology used included aerial photography (scaled and overlain to period 1886 maps and also scaled to match current specific landmarks), survey reference points, and GPS data. The research rendered a specific dirt road that is partially used for recreation today, but other parts are not recognizable as a usable road. Additionally, these period map overlays specifically, and easily, override and contradict roads and paths that many local treasure hunters of the last century have sworn upon.

Sam and Charlotte Clevenger, a cranky old Arizona rancher and his sickly wife, were murdered in 1886. The complete liquidated assets of Sam's life savings, including the sale of his ranch and his livestock, were reduced to gold bullion, then hidden. This story includes the murder, the manhunt, and, more importantly, gold— gold that can be found. The research of this story revealed there is a very high probability this treasure is simply waiting to be found. There is no mention in any court documentation or testimony of the involved individuals that the proceeds of Sam's liquidated assets have ever been found, with exception of approximately $500 Sam carried in his own pocket.

Certainly, the release of this novel will draw some attention to the Buckskin Mountains of Northern Arizona and Southern Utah. If you choose to pursue it, I wish you luck in your hunt for this treasure. The amount of gold bullion is generally unknown, but in my estimation of the rancher's possible liquidated savings, based on his asset sales alone, it is upwards of, if not more than, $5,000 (in 1886). For standard gold bullion in today's value (2016), this raw gold would be valued at close to $330,000. This does not include the antique value of the coins themselves, which could push this to a $1 million-plus payday. If you feel you have the skills and patience to seek real treasure, go get it!

Chapter 1

August 8, 1887
Prescott Prison, Arizona Territory

"If I could jist get my hands on that sum-bitch just fer one minute."

The raspy voice of the cowboy echoed from the prison cell. His dirty and tattered cloths smelled of mildew and sweat. His skinny and bowed saddle legs didn't fill the Levi duck pants like they once did. His facial hair was long and scraggly. For only in his early 30s, he looked like a dripping mess of anxiety.

The chubby guard sat listening in a small wooden chair. He was tilted back against the stucco wall facing the prisoners. The chair creaked and popped as the guard shifted his weight from hip to hip. For a heavier man, this probably wasn't safe. The guard's badge sat tight on his puffed chest. His shirt was missing the top three buttons, and his chest hair bulged out in an attempt to escape. The collar of his shirt was stained from neck sweat along with his rolled sleeves. His face was baby smooth and naturally flush red with dark bagged eyes. He chuckled at the voice he had just heard. The guard's hands continuously wrapped and pulled at a rope with a freshly tied hangman noose. Tying and retying while counting the thirteen wraps of his hangman noose out loud was meant to make prisoners crawl in their skin. Playing with the short piece of rope was a habit for the guard, and taunting was his way of passing the time.

The cowboy placed another card face down. He spoke to himself quietly enough so that no one could hear his words. "Frank, hold it now. Hold it together now. I got this."

His sweat was now pouring down the bridge of his nose from under the brim of his hat. The prison cell was hot and the air was full of sick odors of prisoners. The smell of urine mixed with smokers' coughed air and stale chewing tobacco spit was ripe enough to gag a maggot. Not even a slight breeze slipped through the barred windows. Stuttering a little, the cowboy, Frank, spoke very quietly, but a little louder this time.

"La-last card."

This was a card game of life or death. Each man's fate was literally at hand. Each man, ever so clearly, knew the gravity of this game of fate.

A thirty-year-old Negro man, John, with a ragged mustache sat opposite from Frank on his own bunk within the same cell. As the two men glanced at each other, the Negro man's sweaty hands shook. He slowly crouched down to the dusty prison floor. With a quick look up at Frank, the shaken Negro placed his palm over the seven tattered cards piled one on top of another. He had barely touched them when a chill shot through his body. Trembling, he paused, and in a very nervous and awkward crouch, he tried to speak. "I'm…"

Whatever John wanted to say didn't clear his lips. Quickly removing his hand from the cards, he leaned to his right and vomited violently against the cell wall. Beads of sweat turned to rivers of perspiration running down John's brow. Both prisoners, equally terrified, sat with nearly uncontrollable fear. They both knew for some time what awaited them, but now the realization of raw justice was eminent in each breath they took. Wiping off his mouth with the torn sleeve of his shirt, John watched as the cowboy across from him followed suit with a heave of his own, but was able to retain the expulsion.

Frank coughed a few times and wiped his own mouth with the back of his hand. John closed his eyes tightly and positioned himself against the wall, trying to rest his tense body. His five-foot-six-inch frame was small, but so were most of the prisoners. The prison food was hardly palatable and came in small portions. Salted sawdust would have filled his stomach better. John's mulatto complexion was dirt smudged. His boney cheeks were covered with a young man's skin with traces of wire-black hairs not ready to become a beard. The sparse and curly mustache looped into his upper lip. Bloodshot eyes seemed to be on the verge of bursting with tears at any second. Some sharp memories darted through his mind. He recalled Fort Thomas, Arizona Territory, and a legendary Indian Wars Army major, Anson Mills. That is where John's life took a turn, landing him in this place and in this particularly disturbing card game.

Chapter 2

February 6, 1886
Fort Thomas, Arizona Territory

"Sir, now if you'll turn in your equipment to this fine private to my left, he'll check your equipment in and you'll receive your discharge, soldier. The United States thanks you for your service."

Major Anson Mills shook John's hand and, with a quick, final signature, sealed John's formal discharge from the U.S. Cavalry. John looked at the document with almost complete relief as he read upside down across the table. Even without a formal education, John could read fairly well compared to most of the company he kept in the military. He had a knack for learning quickly. The document read, "John A. Johnson, Company F, 10th U.S. Cavalry, enlisted 1881, discharged this day of February 6th, 1886."

The enlisted soldier in charge of inventory collections, a Negro, started gathering John's Army-issued equipment, marking a rudimentary checklist as he collected the gear. The major was a very busy man, and his attention was soon diverted to another higher-ranked soldier who took Major Mills outside for a private, unrelated conversation.

The freshly enlisted Negro started on John's issued items list. "Saddle bags, check. Put them over there in the corner by them otherns. Canteen, check. Sword, check. Sidearm...where's your pistol, sir?"

John hesitated only for a moment and convincingly answered, "The Injuns that raided our camp last week, sir, didn't take much else of value, but made off with my six-gun and what little ammo I had."

John knew the private wouldn't question him. Many soldiers had lost equipment to the Apache. Many Indian raiders became armed with modern firearms this way. John was part Negro himself. His mother was a Negro slave and his father was her owner, a white merchant from Maine. John's appearance was that of a full-blooded Negro. He lacked physical features that would lead someone to believe he was only half. Whether the private believed John or not, he was on his side, and whatever John said was good enough for him. John outranked the fresh private, not so much by rank, but by experience.

The private collected the items from John and spoke briefly.

"Sir, I be headin' out after some Apache soon with a bunch of the boys. I hear them Injuns are a mean bunch. You ever kilt an Injun? I'z be aimin' to git me some."

John snickered and responded to the private, "If the Injuns don't gitcha, the heat will, or maybe the notion you think you gonna git them before they'z git you. I hear word this fort doesn't have much use anymore. You'll be all right if they move everyone out, back to Texas if you're lucky." John shrugged and headed out of the major's quarters. The rest of John's personal effects were in a roughly beaded, beaver skin possibles bag. John had scavenged the bag from a dead Sioux Indian back in Kansas on the long trip west.

"John, where you headed?" yelled a soldier who was cleaning the bore of his Springfield rifle.

John looked to the soldier sitting on a straw bale and replied with a large smile, "Going north! Not sure where or when I'll get there, but I'm going. Rather take my chances with the Injuns than one more summer in Arizona Territory. Headin' north a couple miles, up to the Collins Ranch today. Reckon I'll try to find a good horse for the trip."

John jogged over to the soldier, held his friend's left shoulder with one hand, and clinched the other hand in a Texas-style handshake. John said to him with a large smile, "Maybe I'll see you again. You got what it takes to deal with this place."

That was the last John spoke to anyone in the 10th Cavalry. The soldier was one of very few soldiers whom John was on speaking terms with. John was considered a half-breed, still a Buffalo soldier—not white and not Negro. He kept company with few soldiers, but they too often shunned him. The many fights he was in were usually race related. The name placed upon him was the lowest common denominator in the company of Buffalo Soldiers, "Gringo Nigga." This is what set John into a fighting rage without pause. He was not proud of the "fair character" rating he had received on his discharge papers. The proud nature that John emitted did not allow anything to roll off his back. It was probably the reason he held the same rank of private for his entire enlistment. The military was not conducive to awarding ranks to men like John Johnson.

Just a few hours north of the fort, John walked tired and slowly. He cautiously walked evenly paced and methodically. He had been here days earlier returning from his last perimeter scouting excursion. Remembering the area well, he started searching. He recognized where he was and glanced around to verify that no one was around. Picking up on some tracks in the sand at the bottom of a small gully, he ducked and scurried up the small wash. With a few glances behind his shoulder, John slid up to a small Joshua tree and reached his hand into the crook where the tree forked into several arms of sharp, spiny bark. He pulled a pistol, belt, holster, and two boxes of cartridges from the crook in the tree. John had stashed these items days earlier knowing his discharge was soon. He had a small amount of cash, but not enough to cover all his expenses. So in an effort to save money and not have to purchase a weapon, he hid his Colt revolver to avoid turning it back in to the military. Several soldiers had pulled this off, and it seemed like a good idea.

John made a quick fire and laid out a blanket for the night. He shifted into a comfortable low spot in a gully. He was out of the wind in the sandy gravel and under a large Palo Verde tree, and soon he drifted off to sleep.

The next morning, he resumed his direction on the main trail that followed the Gila River north to the Collins Ranch. The Collins Ranch was known for selling horses and mules to discharged soldiers for somewhat of a discount.

When John arrived at the ranch, he spotted the rancher throwing grain to his chickens. The rancher's dog began barking as John walked into the rancher's view from beyond the chicken coop.

"Morning, sir," he said loudly to the rancher to overcome the barking dog and the loud, hungry chickens scampering about the rancher's feet.

"Mornin'. I saw you on the ridge earlier. You must be a Buffalo discharge. You come from the fort?"

John nodded. "Yes, sir. I hear you have a good stock of horses and I'd like to buy one."

The rancher's large, three hundred-pound frame was complemented by a smile larger than life. He answered in a chuckle, "Mu name's J. B. Collins. You can call me Jay, J. B., or Collins, or whatever'n hell you want. I respond to noise, tongue lashin's, and butt whippin's! Hehehe! Let's you n' me take a walk. I'll show you what we got and you can pick for yourself."

John smiled with an uncomfortable smile, not certain of what J. B. had just said. John responded, "How do you keep your horses from the Indians? Sure seems everyone has problems with the Apache stealin' stock."

J. B. nodded as he giggled some more, then wiggled his finger toward a small wood-slat building. "See that there? Let's go have a look-see."

Before reaching the building, it was clear why J. B. proudly wanted to share.

"Ya see, when it gets later in the afternoon, we gather up all the stock and put 'em in my corral yonder. If my boy, Dubins, makes any noise at night, we slip over here behind my honey-gun, then let them Injuns have it."

"Gatlin gun! How'd you come across one of these?" John's voice was a little excited.

"Traded a bunch of horses for it, back when the Army was at Camp Grant. We figured they needed the stock pretty bad. Hell, we didn't even raise no cattle till we got this beauty. Makes it real tough for them Apache to do me any harm. You see them trees—top of the ridge yonder? We string up the dead ones for the rest to see. Let them 'paches know we ain't foolin'. Coyotes and crows get 'em down after a week er two."

John winced at the graphic way the rancher described his security measures. "Yeah, I guess that'd keep me away, sir," he muttered quietly. He leaned with his arms through an uncovered window at the rear of the small shed fortress.

It was midday and warming. J. B. offered John some water and he politely accepted. Drinking from the battered tin mug, John pointed to the fenced pasture that contained a small herd of about five horses.

"I ain't got much to spend. What you got for a poor fella that's just lookin' for a ride?"

J. B. chuckled and rubbed his huge, stiff belly up and down as he spoke. "I'll give you a hell of deal on one o' them there Indian horses. Them few painted mares yonder were a gift from the last bunch of Apaches that came through, if you know what I mean. We'll git that stocky brown and white one in. You can take her."

J. B. puckered his lips, squeaked three times, and finished with a high-pitched dog call. "Dubins! C'mon, boy! You git on over here."

Dubins was an old red heeler. As the happy dog loped up to his owner, J. B. leaned down and scratched under the dog's ears. "Double-yew is his name, like the letter ya know, but we like Dubins...don't we, boy? Yes, we do!"

It was very evident the rancher had a very close kinship with the heeler. It seemed for a moment John wasn't involved in the silent, telepathic conversation between the two. The dog's eyes closed halfway and his nubby tail wagged quickly as he enjoyed the scratching and intense attention he was receiving. "Let's you n' me git them Paints for this fine young man. Ain't nobody else wants a damned ol' Indian pony anyhow."

J. B. spoke to Dubins as if he were human, and a close friend. As he muttered a few unrecognizable, subtle commands, the dog listened carefully, then bolted to the field and slowly rounded up the few horses. Only a few short minutes later, the horses were trotting in circles, with Dubins nipping at their heels, around the inside edge of the corral. John and J. B. had walked to the open gate. They closed the corral with Dubins guarding the opening until the gate was latched.

"I'll take her. She looks like a fine horse. Yep, that brown and white mare."

John dug in his beaver bag and handed J. B. some coins and thanked him. "Will that do it?"

"Yep, that'll do."

"Say, you alone out here or you got some family?"

The rancher's face went serious and the smile faded. "Nope, just me 'n Dubs here. I had me a good lady who was better than any cattleman I ever did see. She rode out for supplies with my son to St. Thomas a few years back. Haven't seen 'em since. Apache were real nasty back then. Not much better now, but Injuns 'round here been learnin' a bit of respect, if you know what I mean."

John glanced back to the building that held the Gatlin gun and munitions. "Yes, sir, I gotcha. You got yourself quite the setup. I have to say, I ain't never seen a dog work like that neither, sir."

Leaning down and reaching his hand out to pet the dog, he was briefly taken aback when the old heeler started growling deeply. Dubins' hair rose up on his back. The dog slowly backed up behind his owner's right leg.

"Oh man, I 'pologize for Dubins' attitude. He don't take to strangers much. He ain't never seen a man of your color—just somethin' 'boutch ya'll. He'll be OK. Them teeth ain't as mean as they look. The only thing ol' Dubs ever bit is the legs of some lazy stock."

With a smile, John laughed a bit. "That's fine. Maybe it only takes a night or two sleeping in the brush to start smellin' like a song dog."

John thanked J. B. for the conversation and handed him back the empty tin cup. J. B. set the cup on a fence post and headed into the corral to retrieve the horse.

"Where can I pick up some tack? I need a saddle, bridle, and a new bedroll."

J. B. grew that big smile again, then whipped up an intricate rope bridle in what seemed to be under a minute. He slipped it over the mare's nose and ears.

"This ought to get you by till you find some tack. I'd have you head up to Sam's place for some tack over yonder, other side of the dam there, but he's bent outta shape somethin' mean. I bought his irrigation ditch and water rights. Sam figured I got the better end of the deal. I thought $500 was fair, but he stomped off all pissin' and moanin' anyhow. He jist an ol' tired rooster, all crow and no fight left. Don't mind him no nevermind. Now you get on outta here. Head to Safford, that's yer best bet for a full rig. Me and Dubs got some chores piled up 'fore it gets dark."

Using his fingers, John combed the mare's white mane downward. It seemed to stand up just behind her ears. Nevertheless, he was more than satisfied with the mare. She seemed to have a habit of thrusting her nose upward with the bridle placement. Maybe she was somewhat discomforted by the halter, but this didn't bother John. Being a teamster, John had plenty of experience with horses and figured this habit easy to break with a different bridle and bit. The stocky shoulders and rump of the horse was strength John liked, and he knew this horse would have some pack ability.

The two men, now finished with their business, shook hands and parted ways.

John mounted the mare bareback and took J. B.'s advice. He headed south to Safford. Safford was the closest town to find horse tack. The trip took him backtracking past Fort Thomas again, but it was really the only option and the Gila River was easy water.

After a twenty-six-mile ride along the Gila River, John reached Safford. He spent a few minutes to have a drink and some beans at a local saloon. A man was posting a wanted poster on the exterior of the saloon wall near some other postings of the local nature: a town dance poster, mercantile advertisements, etc. John asked the man politely, "I'm looking for some tack for my horse. Do you happen to know who best to talk to?"

"Joshua Bailey. If you need it, Josh gots it. If he ain't gots it, you don't needs it."

John laughed a bit and smiled. "OK, I think I've got you pinned. With a pitch like that, I'm guess'n there's a chance you's him?"

Joshua pinched the rolled cigarette from his mouth. "Yep, you got me. I run the trading post. Collect the mail too."

His clean-cut mustache and bolo hat gave him a distinguished look. Joshua guided John to his store, not far from the saloon. John was thinking to himself, "I'm outta here if the snake oil sales pitch starts in."

While moseying to the store, Josh continued the conversation. "I try a bit of everything. My wife helps with the store, my son helps with the mail, and I try to do just about everything else. See that wagon yonder? I even volunteered to rebuild that for an old man. Kind of an ornery old sap, and rude as hell. I can't complain much—well, maybe a little. Old codger is fairly wealthy. He bought a full team of horses and all new leather riggings. Says he's movin' his kin to Washington State. He done had it with the Apache, I guess."

John quickly raised an eyebrow to the information. "Where can I find the ol' man? I'm getting things together to head north myself."

"He's a tough one to get along with, but suit yourself. He's from up on the river, northwest of Thomas. His name is Sam. Samuel Clevenger. Got's an ol' lady named Charlotte. Don't think I ever seen that gal. Sam says she is sickly with the TB. He gots a daughter too. Jessie. Quiet girl. She don't say much. Sam's supposed to be down to pick up his wagon and the full rig next week." John pointed out that he needed the used saddle standing up on its horn near the counter. John was not picky. He looked it over and had no problems with the saddle. Joshua had the leather handy to make the bridle John requested and could attach it to a new bit of his choice.

"Gonna take me a few days to get my things together to get you a bridle made. I'm just a bit short on time," Joshua said.

John didn't have an issue with the timing. He was bound and determined to meet this old codger when he returned to pick up his wagon. He mumbled to himself as he looked on, "Not your average rancher 'round here has the money to rebuild a wagon and buy a complete rig with horses to boot."

Nine days rolled by rather quickly. Though the wait was much longer than expected, John fell into a job helping a local build a small corral for stabling horses while he waited for the old man to arrive. It was this day that he met Samuel Clevenger.

Joshua finished the leatherwork and found John hanging the gate on its hinges of the newly built corral.

"John, the old man's here to pick up his gear."

John had a quick conversation with his employer and collected his pay for the few days he'd worked. It was clear to Joshua that John had intentions of hiring on with Sam to head north. After a short trot back to Joshua's store, Sam and John made eye contact. John was immediately intimidated by the old man's expression, peering at him over his shoulder with one eye half winked. Sam's large spoon ears tipped forward off his lean and slender skull. His thick eyebrows hung low, shading his squinted and very suspicious, tiny eyes. John glanced at Sam's expensive, very properly tucked outfit. He had not seen a stripe-vested man like this since he was back East as a youngster. The shiny railroad pocket watch chain was not to be missed, nor the exact gig line and fitted nature of Sam's shirt and pants. John spoke confidently and loudly. "John Johnson, sir."

Sam glanced up at John, noticing, but not acknowledging him while making an inspection circle around his newly rebuilt wagon. Sam sniffed deeply as he stood up straight puffing his chest outward, "What the hell do you want?"

John, somewhat ready for the attitude, said, "I hear you're headed up north. I'd like to offer my services as a teamster. I was recently discharged from Thomas and I'd..."

Sam interrupted, "You know anything about cattle or horses?"

"I'd be glad to run your team. I can help with your cattle, but I'm no cowboy. Reckon I could pick it up pretty quick, if'n you'll give me a go at it."

After Sam finished his inspection, he replied, "Aw, what the hell. Don't expect me to pay you anything other than the food you'll eat. We'll see if you can really drive a team. These here horses are a bit green. Joshua couldn't get me anything better. Conniving salesman. He'll stroke ya till you smile, then jab ya in the pocketbook when you least expect it."

The next morning the two set out together. They headed back to Sam's ranch to gather up his family and belongings for the long journey north. John figured that the three-day ride back toward Thomas would give him a solid opportunity to show Sam a thing or two about training a team of green-broke mares.

Chapter 3

August 1887
Prescott Prison,
Arizona Territory—Cold Fate

A large drop of sweat fell from the cowboy's nose and splashed the floor of the cell. A small plume of dust puffed upward. The game was on. Frank and John stared at the cards resting at their feet. The sour smell of vomit now filled the cell. The sound of footsteps slowly strolling closer broke the two men's concentration. John slid his seven cards face down under his bunk. Frank did the same and stuffed the remainder of the deck between the bunk and its steel frame. The steps of the guard turned into a beat. He began to whistle a very slow and eerie version of "Dixie." Approaching the cell, he turned and faced the bars between him and the prisoners with his head tilted down. He stared from under his eyebrows directly at John. "Dixie" was the song of the devil from a black man's perspective. The demeaning bigotry burned deep within his soul.

The guard's whistle turned into slow-spoken lyrics: "Look away, look away, look away, Dixieland." Then he quietly added, "Look away, look away, look away Niggaman."

He then spoke directly to John. "Nigga boy, I hear sometimes the head comes clean off ifn' the rope's a bit long. I ain't never seen it, but I aim to make this rope of yern a bit lengthy. You know, just to see what happens."

Frank stood up with a forced, slight smile and walked to the front of the cell as he joined in. "Yeah, I heard that before. I also heard that you piss yourself and yer eyeballs come poppin' out." This drew the attention of the guard.

"Who in hell asked you? If'n I wanted to hear from you I'd say so," the guard snapped at the cowboy.

All three men stood close with only the cell bars separating the two prisoners and the guard.

The guard leaned into Frank through the cell and grabbed the bars, laughing out loud, "Ha ha, you poor sons-o-bitches!"

He turned to leave when Frank reached out and grabbed the Mexican double loop pistol holster on the guard's right side. The revolver didn't come loose, but the guard was pulled off balance. With a quick jerk, the guard slammed into the bars and dropped the noose-tied rope that he had so proudly displayed. Before he could react, Frank reached through, pulled the guard's hair with both hands, and, without mercy, racked the head of the guard against the cell bars repeatedly. The guard was nearly unconscious when the weight of his body forced Frank to let loose. The man fell to the ground. Moaning and bleeding from several blunt-force gashes on his head, he crawled away down the hall in shame.

Prisoner harassment was not tolerated, and this incident would not be spoken of. The guard would surely be reprimanded for not following policy and not being alert to his distance from a prisoner. Frank closed his eyes and sat back on the bunk. Flashes of violence from his past raced through his mind. A clear memory of an old man's white hair mixed with blood sizzling on the rocks of a fire pit stained his mind. He laid back and rubbed his eyes. His thoughts continued, and in his moment of recollection, he went back to yet another prior incident: a bloody day in Mexico.

Chapter 4

February 18, 1886
Parral, Chihuahua, Mexico

Two drifters arrived in Parral, Chihuahua, Mexico, on the same day. Near the edge of town was a common water trough used by travelers upon arrival. Both men had arrived within minutes of each other. The younger of the two men, Frank, cautiously introduced himself to the older traveler. "Frank Willson, sir. You look a bit rough. Long trip, I reckon?"

Without looking at Frank, the traveler replied, "Rough? What the hell's that supposed to mean?" The older man slipped the bridle off his sorrel mare as the horse leaned into the trough for a drink. As he stroked the horse's mane. The older man was no gentleman. One shirt tail was hanging out, the other was poorly tucked. The shirt had splatter stains from what appeared to be a mixture of gravy, whiskey, and chewing tobacco drool. His handlebar mustache was the only manicured item in his appearance that was noticeable. The man was larger, meaty and thick. His bone structure resembled an ox when compared to a horse.

Frank was much different, and this came to Frank as he inspected this old man. Frank was slender and muscular. Thick chest and strong, fat biceps. Frank had sharp cheekbones and shaved frequently. This old man hadn't shaved his chin or neck for what seemed to be weeks. Frank never allowed his shirt collar to be anything but folded correctly, and he always buttoned all but the very top button. He thought it felt strange when both sides of his shirt became untucked out of order. To see such a torn-up old man reminded him of how good he may have looked when compared.

Frank rolled his sleeves, but his cut forearms were deeply tanned and complemented his overall posture. The girls always liked Frank. It was his frequent bouts with the law and petty fights that pushed them away. He was secretive. No one person really knew any details of his past, just windows of the time they may have known him before he drifted away. Whether he had been married, kids, or always on the move, this was all a mystery deeply protected within only Frank.

The old man looked at Frank from the corner of his eye, spit a long stream of tobacco across the ground, smiled, and spoke with a deep, graveled voice. "Dave Rudabaugh. Who you runnin' from, Willy? Ain't no white man comes down this far into Mexico for any other reason, less he's runnin' from somethin'."

"Frank Willson, sir. It ain't Willy. You can call me Frank, and yeah, I had what you would call a minor dispute with a lawman up in Arizona Territory. Bit of an accident, but the locals didn't see it that way.

"I like Willy. Believe I'll be callin' you Willy from here on out."

"Suit yourself then. From the looks of your ragged mug, you gotta be that Dave from Missouri that Mr. Earp was trackin'. You smell like a damned mangy old dog too."

Frank knew of this Rudabaugh and was a bit excited the minute Dave introduced himself, but Frank's excitement was more financially driven than Dave knew. Dirty Dave was more popularly known to pay his partners in crime very well. His crimes were well known throughout the West. Murder, train robberies, and extortion were his specialties, but he was quite loyal to anyone willing to help his financial standing. The public knew him as "Dirty" Dave Rudabaugh because he didn't take much to bathing.

By now it was late afternoon and the sun had started its dip toward the horizon. The men finished watering their horses and slowly made their way to a nearby abandoned shed. Picking out a shady wall, Dave and Frank sat comfortably on some chopped firewood near the building. As their conversation thickened, Frank pulled out a bottle. "Sir, you like whiskey? Here you go." Frank handed Dave the full bottle of whiskey he had bought near the border a week earlier. He had been packing it for such an occasion.

Frank questioned Dave about the stories that he'd heard as he drifted from town to town throughout Texas and Southern Arizona. After a few swigs of whiskey, Dave soon became very loud. Obnoxiously loud. He loved the attention and celebrity-like status Frank saw in him. Frank was successful in confirming firsthand information regarding the past of Rudabaugh and the huge amount of money he carried with him. Dave had a tendency to talk a bit too much, especially after a few swigs of whiskey, but he easily kept Frank's attention. "I'll tell you 'bout Ol Earp. That sum-bitch done rode his horse half dead tryin' to git me locked up, or hung. I made it here to Mexico this time, but only by a few strides."

Slurring now, Dave continued with his drunken story. "I'd prefer to just sit and wait it out, suck down some tequila, but Earp gots better eyes than me and I know when I've been bested. I can't say the same for some of my men. Few of them is rottin' in the chollas, guts full of buckshot."

Dave and Frank became well acquainted as evening drew near. Each man was somewhat happy to see a white man so far from their home country. Conversations in English were tough to find so far into Mexico. The men finished the bottle of whiskey and slowly strolled into town, leading their horses to the local cantina.

Dave still insisted on calling Frank "Willy." He always had a way of talking down on others; an off-the-cuff nickname was usually just the beginning. It was a way of portraying his self-elevated position in the pecking order. Frank didn't like it, but he knew Dirty Dave's reputation and a quarrel was not what Frank wanted.

"*Camarero!* Hey! *Muchacho! Dos tequillas, rapido!*" Dave dug out some coins and tossed them up on the bar.

"Let's play some poker, Willy." Dave then leaned into Frank's shoulder and spoke quietly. "You see them *hombres* there? I got a bit of a quarrel with one of them. Damn leather-skin beat me to some easy loot couple weeks back. I'm figurin' on gettin' back what was comin' to me. Look there, he's the one with them gawd-awful, noisy ringin' spurs."

Frank, clearly nervous, quietly answered, "Sure, Dave. I ain't much of a poker player, but I can hold my own for a spell, I reckon." Dave clearly had an agenda that Frank really wasn't certain needed his participation. Frank's mishap in Arizona was truly an accident. He had never participated in anything other than a few juvenile fistfights in his younger years. This evening would prove to be Frank's initiation into the world of true outlaws.

The cantina was rundown, dark, and dirty. The two men stumbled to one of the three small poker tables. Dave and Frank soon were deep into a heated game with four Mexicans who were very heavily armed, two of whom wore bandoliers nearly full of .45-70 caliber rifle cartridges crossing their chests. The third Mexican had larger .45-90 caliber rifle cartridges not only in crossing bandoliers, but another pack of this ammunition in a belt-mounted, U.S. Cavalry-marked Rock Island Arsenal leather cartridge pouch. Frank knew this was likely stolen from the U.S. cavalry by means of a border raid or possibly third-hand from an Apache raider near Texas. The men were playing across a mounding heap of Morgan silver dollars and a few gold coins. This was more money than Frank had ever seen all at one time. Not what one would expect in Mexico. This wasn't a game of small peso denominations.

More than an hour passed before Dave started eyeballing Frank. Frank saw a change in Dave and knew something was quickly brewing in Dirty Dave's skull. Before Frank had time to assess the situation any further, Dave slid back in his chair from the card table, rested his right thumb on the grip of his Colt Dragoon pistol, and quietly, but sternly, scorned the Mexican bandit sitting directly across from him. "You. Yeah, you. You cheatin' son of a bitch! I seen yer partner there deal that ace from south of the deck. I reckon you n' me is gonna throw down 'bout now." True or untrue, it was going to get ugly. This statement cleared the cantina of the few patrons who sat at the bar and nearby card tables. One player stood up and backed off. Each man had quite a large sum invested in the current hand at play, so it was going to take a bit more action to separate the remaining four players from their seats.

Slowly reaching for his Remington rolling block carbine, the bandit tried to explain. "No, *senor*. Dis *hombre* by me here, I not know him. *No conozco este hombre!*"

Dave's temper flared. The bandit kept talking. "You making big mistake, *senor*. That gun you have there, veeeery big and heavy. I get my rifle here *vamanos* and…" Before finishing his broken English mock of Dave's choice of sidearm, Dave skinned the giant revolver from its leather and, without hesitation or conscious thought, shot a hole through the bandit's forehead.

The deafening concussion shook the walls, releasing dust from the dilapidated ceiling, clouding the rundown cantina with dust and smoke. Dave, the cowboy playing to the bandit's right, and a stocky Mexican to the left of Dave stood frozen just long enough for the shock to reside and the body of the bandit to slam down hard on the dirt floor. The stocky Mexican reached back behind him, snatched a Sharps carbine, and pointed it at Dave. The Mexican shuffled backwards toward the front door, maintaining eye contact with Dave while trying to slip out before being gunned down.

Dave yelled at the Mexican, "Where the hell are you goin'?" Dave's Colt, still smoking at the muzzle, was now pointed at the Mexican's chest. "Git outta here."

As the stocky Mexican tried to lift the muzzle of his Sharps, Dave yanked the trigger and blasted. Two holes ripped through the Mexican's bandoliers and through his chest. Dave's huge Colt Dragoon was quite loose in the cylinder from years of Rudabaugh abuse, and it had cross-fired into an adjacent cylinder, causing two rounds to fire. Dave grinned an evil smile as the large Mexican flew back into an empty table. For a moment, the only sound that could be heard was the ringing of a spinning Mexican spur.

"Willy, gimmie a hand. Git these dead sons-o-bitches' money and let's get on outta here." The dealer remained frozen in his seat, his hands shaking uncontrollably, still clutching the deck of cards as if still ready to deal. Dave pushed the end of his hot pistol barrel deep into the cheek of the dealer. "Calm down, dammit! You're making my friend here nervous. I know you didn't do nuthin'. Just sit there till we're gone or I'll send you straight to Purgatory with both yer *amigos* here. *Comprendo* Purgatory, *muchacho?*" As the dark tobacco juice dripped from Dirty Dave's large mustache, his crazy-eyed glare slowly shifted to Frank.

"Willy, let's move on out. I reckon we ain't welcome here no more." Frank had frantically rifled through each of the dead men's clothing. He had gathered quite a large sum of currency consisting of Mexican and American bills and coins. He slipped a boot off the first dead man and then used the man's sock to stash the money. Dave looked around cautiously and walked quietly out the back door with Frank following close behind. Dave whispered, "Willy, slip around front and grab the horses."

With a quick snap, Frank answered with a stern whisper, "Hell, no! You get the damn horses—they're right out there in the street. You don't think them Mexicans have their pals waitin' for us to stroll out the front door and catch a belly full o' lead?"

Dave grabbed Frank by the back of his neck and forced him forward. They both shuffled to the edge of the building and peeked around, only to realize that neither of their horses were there. "Damn bandits. Let's git over to the stable there, see if there's some horses. I got a gut feelin' we need to git outta here quick."

Frank agreed. Both men quickly crouched and jogged quietly to the barn wood stables, about a hundred yards from the cantina. As they rounded the first corner of the building, a Mexican had just finished buckling his belt after urinating a large puddle of rendered-down tequila. The men were instantly exposed, and the Mexican made eye contact with Dave. Dave quickly flipped his large Dragoon from its holster, flopped the pistol over, and, with the barrel in his hand, swung a large circular arc outward with the grip end of the gun. Just as the Mexican opened his mouth to alert his amigos, the heavy gun smashed into his right cheekbone, just below his eye. A mist of blood sprayed into the air. The blow was so extreme that the Mexican was dead before hitting the ground, splashing in his own mess. A large piece of the pistol's grip broke loose on impact and was sticking out of the dead man's face. Dave holstered his gun and looked down. The dead man's fingers twitched and contracted, as if trying to grab something. Dave was clearly disgusted that the grips on his beloved Colt were now damaged.

Frank and Dave ran from building to building to reach the stables up the street. They peered through the wooden slats to see that no horses were in the stable to be taken, only some Mexican cowboys sleeping on some broken bales of straw. Dave motioned to Frank and pointed to some horses in a corral on the other side of the stables. "Must be their horses there," Dave said. "Let's go."

They then ran quickly around the end of the building to the corral and quietly started to saddle two of the horses, when out of nowhere, a bullet struck a corral post, spraying splinters against Dave's shoulder. One of the cowboys was awakened by the sound of the horses shuffling about and two men trying to steal them. As soon as the excited cowboy fired a shot from his pistol, the other three Mexican cowboys awoke and gathered their guns to join in.

Frank was a bit quicker than Dave and had the saddle on the horse he rustled. Dave dropped the tack and ran for cover, dropping the sock of money. Frank mounted up and kicked the mare as he ducked low to avoid the whistling .45 slugs. The mare jumped the pole gate and ran into the darkness on the road headed north, out of town. Frank had one last glance at the money he'd just dropped, but the gunfire gave him no notion to turn back to retrieve it. Dave drew his large Colt and ran for cover. The cowboys were near the front doors of the stable facing the street. With no other buildings or cover away from the cowboys, Dave ran to the rear of the stable and then continued back to the cantina. "If any you Mexican sum-bitches in there, best say so now!"

Inside the cantina the bartender stopped cleaning the blood- and entrails-splattered floor when Dave yelled. The bartender yelled out, "¡No problem, senior! I in here! I just keep out of your way, OK?" He then hunkered down and hid motionless with his sawed-off shotgun behind the opened back door, just inside the cantina. As Dave rounded the corner through the door, the bartender recognized the large Colt Dragoon, leading Dave back inside. The bartender yelled with fear "AH!" and jerked both triggers on his double-barreled twelve-gauge Remington. His scream continued through the blasts. The dual charges of buckshot ripped a large hole through the door and struck Dave directly above the shirt collar in his neck. The nerves in Dave's fingers caused them to snap open, and the huge Colt Dragoon slammed to the dusty floor. Dave gurgled and his mouth opened and closed as it failed to release any words. Blood and spit ran down his chin, and his brown teeth were now deep red.

Dave's body fell hard, his limbs twisted in a bloody pile. The bartender's yell switched to some high-pitched whines, then to some deep sighs of relief. He was grabbing Dave by his hair to drag him out the back door when he realized the dead man was completely decapitated by the massive blast from the Remington. In shock, the bartender barked out, "*¿Que demonios?*"

He dropped Dave's severed head and shouted again in Spanish to the Mexican cowboys as they ran for the cantina, still shooting aimlessly in his direction. "Stop shooting, *amigos*! I shot him dead!" The crowd of Mexicans cheered.

It was morning before the town folk had the confirmation that it was the famed Dirty Dave Rudabaugh that the bartender had killed. Yes, the man who had terrorized the town of Parral each time he passed through causing this type of trouble was his trademark. Dave spent time working on several cattle ranches near Parral, but did this as a front for his cattle rustling operations. A frequent visit to town to cause unrest was an understatement. The town was all too tired of Dave pistol whipping a cantina patron if Dave lost a card game, or his occasional beating of a whore due to a financial misunderstanding. Dave needed to go and, for the town of Parral, today was as good as any.

The citizens of Parral mounted Dave's head on a pole and paraded through the streets, cheering the death of the famed villain.

This was another testament of Frank's destiny. Unplanned and unwanted. He fell into trouble yet again. This was so often in Frank's life, he felt trapped in a well of circumstances with no rope out. Frank was frustrated. He thought to himself, "Who would have thought, escaping from Mexico? This was the land of escape, right? This is the end-game for so many outlaws. Where the hell do I go next?"

Frank narrowly escaped Parral and was riding fast to the north. His experience with Dirty Dave Rudabaugh put him on a hard, fast ride out of Mexico in fear of being followed. With no real destination in mind, Frank rode hard back to Arizona.

~~~~~~ *Chapter 5* ~~~~~~

February 20, 1886
Graham County, Arizona Territory

essie Clevenger was fifteen years old. Her adopted father, Sam, had hardened her as more of an employee than as a daughter, and he did not treat her as a female in any respect. She didn't spend time grooming her hair, and she no array of dresses to wear or sewing days with her stepmother, Charlotte. She didn't spend time with friends, nor did she have any. The closest town was all too far, and she was home schooled by Charlotte.

Jessie was more than an exceptional work hand. The few ranch cowboys and travelers who passed through the years were always quick to mention Jessie's striking big eyes, dark thin eyebrows, and overall beauty. She had a mesmerizing stare that caught many young men tripping on their tongues. Jessie looked much older than her seasoned fifteen. Her life did not allow for childhood, or even that of a school-aged girl. She was adopted at eight years old and transitioned directly to an adult with the Sam Clevenger ranch hand training program. Her real parents were killed by former slaves, Negros, so the foster home said. It wasn't unheard of for these foster homes to secretly adopt out children born out of wedlock from prestigious families, or unpredicted pregnancies by prostitutes. The Negro story stopped questions and painted a heartfelt tale for those looking to adopt. Jessie didn't remember anyone she knew of as her real parents, just the foster home and the stories she was told that became her reality.

About a half mile from the ranch house, and near the pond, Jessie stopped digging for a moment. She stabbed her shovel into the bank of muddy grass piled to her side. She paused work to observe the pond and irrigation network her family had built and maintained. The dike that held the pond was in excellent shape, and she took pride knowing she had been able to maintain such a structure without any repairs due to poor construction. This was a good time of year to clear the silt and grass that built up near the irrigation gate and in the earthen ditches. Varmints like gophers and muskrats frequently dug holes through the ditches, causing floodwater to wander in unwanted areas.

Although Sam had recently sold the irrigation system and the ranch itself, Jessie was given the task of finalizing a tributary ditch that rerouted some water to an adjacent field. Both ranches were adjacent to each other and abutted the Gila River. In late January her adopted father, Samuel Clevenger, had sold the neighbor, J. B. Collins, the dam and the irrigation water rights. This was just one of Sam's steps in the inevitable departure of Arizona he had been planning for months.

Jessie was bitter about this work. Samuel was somewhat of a slave driver and usually barked orders in lieu of a polite alternate request for work to be done. She thought the neighboring parcel owner should have to clean out his own ditch, but Samuel loved giving orders, and Jessie wasn't one to complain. As were many western women.

It was early afternoon when she finished clearing the floodgate of the silt and debris from the long stretch of ditch. "If that old bastard would do some of this himself," she mumbled, "he wouldn't be moaning about how long it takes." She grabbed the shovel at the top of its handle, pulled it from the mud, and dragged it back to the house. Jessie expected a fresh set of orders from Samuel, or some small, meaningless line of work from Mrs. Clevenger upon returning. Just as Jessie dropped the shovel handle against the porch post, and before she could crack open the front door of the ranch house, Charlotte Clevenger immediately began moaning from her rocking chair in the living room. Coughing a little and wiping the speck of blood from her lips. she gestured to Jessie. "Jessie, get me some water, honey."

The old woman was frail. The tuberculosis seemed to be advancing at a much faster rate to Jessie. Sam moved her and

Charlotte to Arizona per the doctor's recommendations for a dry climate. Charlotte was needy and helpless. Not in the sense of a sickly person, but she was always this way, particularly with Jessie. Charlotte's face was old, wrinkled, and skinny. Her face was thin and the shadow of her skull could nearly be seen through her clear, pale blue skin. Her sunken eye sockets were a constant reminder to Sam and Jessie that she was not well and not long for this life. Her body was frail and boney. Charlotte chose the puffy dress she wore specifically to add bulk to her frame and to keep warm.

Without speaking, Jessie frowned and stomped around the house to take care of Mrs. Clevenger's requests.

Old Mrs. Clevenger knew when she had pushed Jessie's buttons, but only hummed to ignore the noise of the youngster's feet on the wood floor and hardly made eye contact to avoid the stern scowl that accompanied Jessie's frustration. The humming was an added irritant that Jessie despised. All the small things just added up to one frustration after another.

The Clevengers were quite fed up with the Arizona Territory. Sam and his wife had been discussing off and on about moving out of Arizona before summer arrived. The Indian affairs of the area caused ongoing problems for all homesteaders and ranchers, but the heat was also a major concern. Sam had left the ranch a few days back, then headed for Safford to pick up his wagon that was being refurbished. Mrs. Clevenger had no knowledge of Sam's recent ambitious jump to fix equipment and have the wagon rebuilt. This would be a welcome surprise to Mrs. Clevenger. The wagon had been sitting for over a year. The old oak "bucket" (Sam's pet name for the wagon) had endured a tough trip when the Clevengers moved to Arizona, and the dry heat of the West had loosened every board, bolt, peg, and wheel spoke.

Samuel and Charlotte Clevenger's only known photographs as printed in "True Frontier" magazine August, 1974.

John drove the green-broke team of horses in front of the wagon with ease. Sam was quite impressed with John's ability, but he would never express this openly. Sam wore a fancy tailored suit to town, for he was very conscience of his appearance. His fine outfit, wagon, new tack, and fresh horses looked as good (or better) than any in the territory.

Jessie and Mrs. Clevenger watched Sam and John approach the ranch. John struggled a bit as they reached the edge of the meadow. The horses became restless, as horses do when they return home. After only a few minutes trotting up the road, the herd stopped at the corral. Sam was a bit ruffled with the actions of the horses as they reached the corral. The team pulling the wagon greeted their kin by touching noses across the corral rails.

Sam, still a bit shaken by the unexpected trot, scowled. "These damned ol' son's o' bitches. I ought to smack hell out of 'um!" Breathing a little heavier than usual, he wiped the sweat from his bright red face with a handkerchief he had pulled from his suit pocket. Sam's fancy pocket watch had bounced from its pocket and hung low, swinging wildly as he dismounted the wagon.

Mrs. Clevenger yelled at Sam. "What is this? I guess you're set on leaving sooner than I expected?"

Sam coughed and replied, "Yeah, I hired me this nigga boy teamster to drive that good for nuthin' green-broke team of misfits. I need some food, damn it." The tone of his angry voice was plenty to ruffle one's feathers, and the skinny pointer finger that he poked around while talking could be quite irritating.

After somewhat settling down from the trip to town, Sam barked his usual orders to Jessie and Mrs. Clevenger. "Get some meat cooking in the pot. Never mind no shortcuts now. I busted my hump this week for all of us, damn it." Sam liked referring to the "pot" when he mentioned cooking. It was his way of reminding Mrs. Clevenger of the Christmas present he had given her the previous year. She did like the large iron Dutch oven, but it was more of a necessity than a gift, so Sam's reference always caused some discomfort.

Sam continued: "Tomorrow we'll load up everything. I think we can start for Holbrook mighty quick. You women are going to need to get me a solid inventory of our supplies and make damn certain we got what we need to cover some miles. I reconciled and closed up affairs with the bank. Pack plenty of food in the wagon too. I hear Camp Windy has some good fruit due to our mild winter, but I'll be damned if we run outta meat and beans before we get there." As John brushed off his shirt and dismounted the wagon, Mrs. Clevenger shook John's hand with a semi-warm greeting. Jessie was quite shy and didn't have much of a greeting to offer.

Jessie knew only of the stories the foster home taught her about Negroes. She was told that former Negro slaves killed her real parents for retribution of pre-Civil War enslavement and the current segregation at that time. Even though her parents supposedly never owned slaves, they were singled out because they were easy and ripe for the picking. Jessie was also taught that all Negroes were a dirty subversion of humans that God himself stained black for their sins. Jessie was naive, brainwashed by the foster home employees who set aside time to try and further their Confederate-type agenda. Even though the war was over, there was great distaste of Negroes and their newfound freedoms in her foster home. The home would not foster Indian, Chinese, Negro, Mulatto, or any children of the sort. Jessie learned to hate Negroes at the most vulnerable time in her life, and this hate was as part of her as much as the curls in her hair.

Mrs. Clevenger brushed the dust from Sam's shoulders, straightened his crooked collar, and put his watch back into its pocket. "Sam, is this man, John, going to drive all the way up to Washington?" she asked.

Sam walked past Mrs. Clevenger and Jessie to the front doorway of the ranch house as he answered back, "I'm too damned old to drive that team. I'll be damned if we ain't the only ones trying to leave this hot son of a bitch." Mrs. Clevenger shook her head in disagreement with his tone. The last few years in Arizona had hardened Sam. His negativity rubbed off on Jessie, and Jessie tended to follow Sam's lead.

The Clevenger family had long been waiting for the day Sam would step up and get things prepared for the move north. Civil conversation in the Clevenger household was rare. Talking frequently about the notion to try a different part of the West was really the only thing the family agreed upon. Sam had slowly sold off farm equipment and unnecessary, bulky items they did not need for the trip. The Clevenger family was all very serious about the goal at hand. Finally, Sam came through with the final task of delivering the wagon to Safford for a local blacksmith to rebuild and gear up.

The next day came and went quickly. It was a quiet day as they each did their part to load only the most appropriate belongings. On Sunday morning, the family set off at daybreak.

Chapter 6

March 20, 1886
Holbrook, Arizona Territory

Two boys wrestled violently as the third stood laughing. "You shut your bean hole! I gets to be Billy, and you can be Pat! You always git to be Billy!" Alan yelled as he threw Tommy to the ground. The boys couldn't have been more than eight years of age. As they played, the disagreement erupted into a small fight. The wrestling match was at the front steps of the bank while the youngsters waited for their parents to complete their business inside.

Frank Willson had just arrived and strapped his horse to the hitching post across the street. Seeing the rush of dust of the two youngsters slamming each other into the ground, he quickly walked over to stop the scuffle. "Hey, hey now! You two knock it off!" Frank scorned the boys.

Laughing loudly, Alan stood up and delivered Tommy a stiff kick to the kidney as he tried to escape from the ground, not nearly quick enough. Alan had the edge when it came to tact and speed. Frank grabbed him by the hair at the base of his neck. This stopped Alan's cackling laugh quickly.

With tears running down his face, Tommy dusted off his pants and yelled back at Alan, "Gawd damn you! I'm through with you, you son of a…!"

Frank couldn't help but smirk as he stopped the boy's curse. "Hey now, does yer pa know you talk like that?" Tommy turned away with a deep frown and started up the bank steps to fetch his mother. She had missed the whole event.

Alan barked back, "Tommy Tasker, you're a yella'-bellied sap-suckin' sum-bitch!" Frank had a way of trying to help. Standing with Alan's hair in his hand as the boy's father stomped out from the bank did not look so good. "What the hell are you doin' ta mu boy?" Alan's father snapped.

Frank wanted to explain the situation, but didn't have time to start when the rock-solid right hook slammed into his face, landing Frank flat on his back.

"Come on, boy, you git home." With that said, the man and his son turned and started walking away.

And again, Alan had the last word. "Yeah, mister, my daddy will whoop you're ass again if'n you…" The boy's father smacked his side of Alan's head for the curse and they disappeared up the street.

Frank Willson had this type of luck. These misunderstandings happened many times to Frank throughout his life. The false perception that Frank was "no good" was seeded from these run-ins with his fate.

The trouble in Parral with Rudabaugh landed him a few extra dollars to hitch a train ride north. He stayed at a few hotels on his way, but none of these small luxuries were worth the long-term effect on Frank's character. The emotional strain had passed, but the incident had hardened him more than he knew. Holbrook, Arizona, was already making Frank's stomach turn, reminding him of the stress in Parral. Frank always had moments of reflection in these incidents, which took his mind back to the previous bad-luck encounter. Frank held his hand over the side of his cheek. He spoke quietly to himself: "Shake it off—I got this."

He pressed the bruise and nursed the dull pain that engulfed the left side of his face. A teenage girl stood by a porch post in front of the store. She watched Frank over her shoulder, interested. The young lady looked away quickly when he spotted her. His double take caught her looking again. "What chew looking at, Missy?" Frank asked as he tried to shake off the shame of being dropped by a single punch.

She stepped around the rear wheel of the wagon and replied, "I saw what happened, you know. That man done you wrong. If that boy was mine I'd take a willow switch to his backside."

Frank puffed a tiny laugh, smirked a bit, and spat a small bit of blood to the ground. "Yeah, but if I was the boy's pa, I'd a done the same." They stood there for a minute, obviously uncomfortable with not much to talk about. The girl seemed noticeably attracted to Frank due to her flirtatious tone and her stare that drew him in—maybe not as much for his looks, but for the noble action he had taken to try and discipline the boys. It wasn't every day a man could withstand that sort of public abuse with the humility Frank exercised.

"I'm Jessie. We're just passing through. I'm traveling with Sam and Charlotte Clevenger down from 'bout Safford. Charlotte's gotten mighty sick with the TB and we're moving up to Washington. They say it's cooler, but the mountains are so pretty. Charlotte would like to finish what she has left of livin' away from this heat."

Frank answered with his condolences. "Well I always say, don't ever finish with a compromise. If'n your Charlotte wants Washington, then she should get Washington. I plan on meetin' up with the Maker by a nice grove of trees, creekside. I reckon it ought to be someplace where I can listen to clear water ripplin' across some rocks and a cool breeze. 'Course, ain't no place I seen recent like that."

"That sounds so simple, but real nice. I ain't thought much about it. I guess I ain't old enough to worry 'bout such things." She turned away with an uncomfortable smile and walked back to the wagon to finish organizing the canned goods Sam had purchased.

The wagon was parked in front of the general store. Sam Clevenger was inside settling the bill on the new chuckwagon he had purchased along with the supplies to fill it. John Johnson was packing out flour and other miscellaneous larger goods and loading up the chuckwagon. He witnessed the end of the conversation between Jessie and Frank.

John tossed a bag of potatoes on the wagon and got Frank's attention. "You may watch yourself. Her daddy ain't so keen on strangers smiling sweet on her."

Frank walked to the wagon and untwisted a rein on the team of horses. "Name's Frank Willson. Ya'll is headed to Washington?"

"Yes, sir, I'm just a hired hand for this here rig. Mr. Clevenger took me on to help out. We got a pretty nice herd of cattle and horses just outside town."

Frank smiled and asked John, "You look Cavalry with that hat and 'spenders. You cowboy'n this operation too?"

"Tryin', but I had a hell of a time cowboy'n from the Gila River all the way here. The old man needs someone with a bit more experience to help out. Terrain gets a bit precarious, I hear. You interested?"

"Ah hell, I don't know. I've been ridin' railroad and just tryin' to find some opportunity. Texas, Arizona, Mexico…I ain't found nuthin' yet. I reckon I can think on it."

Sam and Charlotte finished their business in the store and returned to the wagon to find the men talking. John addressed Sam. "Sam, this here's Frank. He claims to be a good hand with cattle. I think he might help out. You wanna let him on?"

Sam looked up and down Frank. "Name's Samuel Clevenger and I'm runnin' this operation. You got some know-how and some experience with a mixed herd?"

"Yes, sir. I been cowboy'n off and on since I was a boy. Back in '82 and '83 I ran some longhorn and a few horses on the Chisholm Trail."

A few more short questions and Sam seemed satisfied. From Frank's attire it was clear he was nothing less than a cowboy with real experience.

It was done. Sam, John, Frank, Jessie, and Mrs. Clevenger all introduced themselves further. With light conversation while finalizing the loading operation, it was time for the journey northbound.

The wagons were both filled with fresh sundries and standard supplies. So full, in fact, that items were hung on the sides of the larger wagon, such as water barrels, a shovel, a handsaw, and some miscellaneous ropes.

Sam pulled Charlotte aside and walked to some stocked items back in the store. "Buy this Dutch oven. It's a bit smaller than the pot, but it'll make for easier movin'. I'll be using the big one for somethin' else."

Sam hung the old iron "pot" from a hook at the rear of the wagon. It rode below the floor, gently swinging from its bail as the wagon paraded out of town in a display often encountered in the West—that is, with the exception of the gleaming, newly refurbished wagons. John was leading the team. Charlotte and Jessie sat next to John on the buckboard. Sam rode his old sorrel gelding, leading the mule that pulled the small chuckwagon. Frank rode ahead of the group to gather the herd, which rested near a pond north of town. It was early afternoon when they departed Holbrook.

Chapter 7

April 10, 1886
Near Willow Springs Fort,
Arizona Territory

The Clevengers quickly made a week's worth of travel without incident. They settled in for a week or so of rest just south of Camp Windy. With water and some fresh grass nearby, it was a great location to prepare for another leg of the long journey.

Frank rounded up the herd of horses and cattle near a seep that had just enough water to keep the animals interested for the evening. John set up the camp, greased the wagon hubs, and started a fire. Mrs. Clevenger sat in her rocking chair that Sam finally agreed to bring along. He knew it was one of the items that would keep her complaints to a minimum.

Sam was acting supervisor, walking in a pattern around the wagon, fire, and tents.

"Jessie, you go out there and git Willson. Gettin' dark and I reckon it's time for us to get eatin'. Since John here burnt the last batch of beans, I figure Willson can have a shot at 'em tonight. You worthless kids need a lesson on how it's done."

Jessie dropped the firewood and brush she had gathered. She stomped through the camp right past Sam with a brush to his left arm as her irritation swelled. Sam spun around. "You watch that demeanor, little lady. I'll whoop you with a fresh willa' stick if you get smart with me."

Sam turned and saw John staring up at him from a kneeling position with an uncomfortable stare. Sam snapped back at John immediately. "What the hell you looking at, nigga boy? Get that new iron cookin' pot, the one outta the wagon, and get them beans and bacon goin'."

John snapped back, "Yes, Massa! Anything else I'z kin do fo' ya, Massa?" The comeback was strong and John steamed as he glared at Sam. John didn't speak like this—ever. This was the first time John was ever pushed to talk back to an employer. The military had a zero tolerance of these incidents. Sam kicked the dirt hard and yelled, "Nigga! Get it done now, or get the hell outta here, goddammit!" John reluctantly gathered up the cookware and the larger Dutch oven from inside the rear of the wagon. Some minutes went by and John forced himself to cool his temper.

As John unloaded the heavier, larger cast iron oven, he noticed the "pot" wasn't hanging from its usual spot. "Mr. Clevenger, sir, did we lose the old pot? We ain't hit any rough spots to shake her loose today."

"Damn it! How the hell should I know?" He shrugged and walked off without an answer. Smirking and shaking his head, John mumbled sarcastically, "Unbelievable. Old white man just mad all the time."

While in Holbrook, Sam had organized his finances. Moving north required the unnerving method of carrying his life savings along for the trip. Recent land sale proceeds and his savings were now reduced to bullion in mostly gold eagles. Sam kept the $500 from the irrigation system to the neighbor in St. Thomas in bills and coins for traveling expenses. Sam tucked the money into his pants and suit pockets for his personal safekeeping. The larger sum of money from the sale of the Clevenger ranch, land, cattle, and horses was rendered down to large denominations of gold coins. Sam was very pleased to see the canvas banker bag heavy with shiny $20 gold double eagles. The bank manager made it a point that a handful of the coins were fresh double eagles from the Philadelphia mint and had just arrived this week with the delivery of some other military documents and teller cash.

Sam tasked Charlotte to hide the money in the large iron pot and dispose of the banker canvas bag. She agreed with this and felt even though it was right out in the open all day, it was also very easy to watch. It would hang next to the axle grease bucket, and nobody wants to get near the axle grease. Everyone seemed to be rummaging around for things in the wagon daily, so it was only logical to keep it outside of the regularly stored items within the wagon. With a wire wrapped side to side around the pot as reinforced bail, it secretly held nearly $6,000 in American gold eagles. After nightfall, Sam easily slipped out of camp long enough to stash or bury the pot until morning. Charlotte took a few turns at this job as well. This had been going on without incident or inquiry from anyone since departing Holbrook. Everyone enjoyed the absence of Sam for any short time he wandered away from camp. These walks were after dark and never questioned.

"Hey, wake up, Mugwomp," Frank whispered harshly into John's ear. It was early and the sun hadn't broken the horizon yet.

"Mugwomp—hell is that?" John mumbled back to Frank as he sat up, his eyes still half closed.

"I seen a couple Injuns on the horizon. We gotta git over and see if they plan on rustlin' the stock. They was ridin' north on that ridge."

John's eyes opened quickly and he was now fully awake. Frank pointed to the east, where the morning sun still hid behind the red ledges. John grabbed his belt by the brass buckle and wrapped it around his waist. He took the Colt Single Action Army from its holster, flipped the loading gate, and cycled through the cylinder to verify that every hole was filled. Frank shuffled to the wagon and pulled his Winchester '73 carbine from a scabbard mounted near the buckboard. Frank and John both knew that the Indians saw them from the vantage point high on the ridge looking down into their camp. The terrain was mostly rock, red and gray clay hills with scattered juniper trees, some spotty sagebrush, and not much for cover. John headed to his horse when Frank grabbed him by the back of the shirt. "Nope, you ain't gittin' on that horse. I don't think they know we're up. Let's not make a stir. Besides, there may be more than the two I seen."

Eyebrows up, John nodded in agreement. They both made a quick sprint to the east toward the ridge. After several hundred yards, keeping cover and periodically stopping for a glance around, they made it to the base of the ridge. "Frank, we best be damn careful peekin' over the other side. Them Injuns might o' switched back behind the ridge, then south again to get back to the stock if they figured we was still sleepin' and didn't see 'em." John finished talking and was still breathing heavily from the footrace.

"Yep, reckon they coulda done, sneaky sons a bitches," Frank whispered. They hunched over low and put on a sneak to the summit of the ridge, belly crawling the last twenty yards to peek over.

"Where the hell did you get those?" John asked, just as Frank dug out a pair of new Browning binoculars from within his shirt. "The old bastard down there had 'em stuffed in the chuckwagon." Frank started to put the optics to his eyes for a look just as John barked a whisper. "Right there—see 'em, right there! By that small tree, 'tween the rocks!" Frank had his upper lip curled to his nose as he tried focus through the binoculars. "Hang on, I can't see nuthin'."

John frantically asked, "Do they see us? Are they lookin at us?" Frank was weaving his head left to right, back and forth, clearly not looking in the right direction through the optics.

John started in on Frank. "You don't know how to use them, do ya? Give 'em here. Maybe you is the Mugwomp." Frank struggled for a minute as John grabbed the binoculars from Frank's grip.

Frank was now frustrated with John, his eyebrows stiffening. "Who in hell you callin' Mugwomp? You don't even know what a damn Mugwomp is!"

John was now looking through the binoculars. "They can't see us—looks like they're planning something. Their fingers is in the dirt and they keep pointing in the direction of the herd. Frank, ain't the herd just around that hill south of 'em?" John dropped the binoculars down to look at Frank, who had just flipped up the tang rear sight on his Winchester, already aiming. This alarmed John. "Wait! They gots to be all of two hundred yards. You ain't..."

The rifle discharged before John could finish his sentence. The rifle blast sounded more like a canon echoing down into the draw. The early morning air was crisp, and John's ears began to hum. *Whap!*

The bullet hit hard flesh and bone. One of the Indians clutched his upper thigh after the slug hit high on his leg. He fell hard to the ground with a spin as a heavy stream of blood poured into the sand. The other Indian mounted his horse, pivoted to the south, then pivoted again to the north. It looked as if he was confused and didn't see the black powder smoke before it dissipated into the yellow dead grass. The wounded Indian crawled to a nearby gully that was low enough for Frank and John to lose sight of him.

Frank and John buried their chins in the dirt and froze. The bareback-mounted, skinny, and war-painted Indian kicked his small black and white pony with his color beaded moccasins and began a flat-out run directly at John and Frank. The confused Navajo pointed his lever-action Star carbine into the air and yelped a war cry. There was a healed scar of skin where the Indian's right eye used to be, as an unfortunate accident left him with only his left eye. The rifle was an outdated paper cartridge style, a short single-shot that required a cap to discharge. The Indian retained the loaded round in the rifle for a shot at his enemy, if he could only see who shot his partner. Holding the crude rifle in his right hand, he rode hard, real hard.

Frank and John watched him gallop right to them—and pass by not more than ten yards away. The men were still unseen and hiding low in the short brush and dead grass. The Navajo made another loud battle yell when he topped the ridge, but the scream quickly turned to a drowning gurgle. John had drawn a solid bead with his Colt and drilled a .45 round through the warrior's back, into his left lung. The Indian slowly slid from the horse, falling face-first into a rock pile.

The other wounded Indian who had been hit by Frank's '73 was now firing back at them. The small-caliber pistol was terribly off target and was missing Frank and John by nearly twenty feet in various directions. The shots didn't frighten either of them.

"Put that damn thing away. I can get him with this long gun," Frank snapped at John. John nodded and holstered his Colt.

Frank leaned up to the side of a Juniper tree using it as a dead rest and took careful aim with his Winchester. The Indian lifted his head above the bank for another array of potshots after reloading his small revolver. Frank took a deep breath and fired a single shot from the carbine. One half inch higher and it would have missed. The bullet connected with a lethal blow as it struck the top of the Indian's head, parting his hair, flesh, and bone. The lead slug canoed his skull wide open. Frank nodded continuously in satisfaction for a few seconds. He mumbled to himself, "Sons a bitches."

Frank jogged over to where the dead Indian's horse stood near the body. He grabbed the horse by the reins and mounted the bareback mare. John picked up the Indian's rifle and found four remaining paper cartridges from the Indian's leather pouch about his waist. Frank helped John onto the horse's rump for the ride back to camp. They were both flush with adrenaline and were well aware they had to get moving.

"Frank, gimmie a few bullets," John said.

Frank pulled three .44-40 rounds from his belt and handed them to John. "I saw yer empty box back at camp—I figured you'd be askin' shortly. These ought to shoot in that .45. Bit smaller, but they'll work in a pinch."

John pocketed two bullets, flipped the loading gate on the Colt, rolled the cylinder, ejected the empty shell from the .45, and slid the .44-40 into the empty cartridge hole. He then slapped the gate closed and did a fancy roll with the pistol as he holstered it and secured the U.S.-marked leather flap over the wooden Cavalry grips.

Neither was quite sure if more Indians were in range to hear the skirmish, so a quick "load-n-git," as Frank put it, was in order. Sam had the girls hide in the wagon while he loaded everything in the camp for their quick departure. The shots were noticeably close and everyone was awakened by the blasts. Frank and John mounted their horses and headed back to gather the herd. They would easily make it to Willow Springs Fort before day's end.

The group was in quite a hurry to find their own kind and hold up within the safety of the fort. As their wagon rolled by a small hill entering the last quarter mile to the fort, Sam spoke as he pointed out to Frank the signage that was carved on a flat stone face that read "Camp Windy."

Sam motioned to Frank, "Hey Willson, look yonder. Didn't take a damn genius to figure that one out. This nasty wind been blowin' since Holbrook."

Frank rode his horse closer to the wagon and replied, "Yep, that name scratched in the rock there, Lorenzo Watson, I met him and one of his brothers down near Mexico couple years back. They helped Lee build that Ferry back in the day. 'Course, that was all before the Utah law dragged Lee back to the Meadows and shot him dead, sittin' on his own coffin. Seems them Watson boys was fairly loyal to Lee. Didn't figure on stickin' around here after all the killin' and what-not. Spooked hell outta everyone around here. And that other fella that scratched his name there too, J. Swap, he's from up to Overton settlement. He's easy to spot, always wearin' them huge leather chaps and a red neckerchief. You could slide a whisky barrel 'tween his bowed legs. Thought he'd come here to help with the herd of horses last year. Watson boys told me to watch out for him. He'd nearly beat a horse to death for sneezin' on him. Bit of a temper, I reckon."

Frank winked at Jessie and smiled as he clicked his cheek and pealed his horse back to skirt the flank of the herd. Sam also turned back to ride behind the larger wagon to be in eyeshot of his pot. The history lesson Frank gave to Sam was the most Frank ever spoke to Sam. Jessie was next to John on the buckboard, silent as usual, especially sitting next to John. Her intense stare took Frank back a bit while he spoke. She was not only very interested in the story, but also her interest in Frank was growing daily. After the incident with the Indians, Frank took charge. Sam was rattled, Charlotte was uncomfortable and ever so sick. Frank naturally took the role of protector with John's help. Jessie watched this change in Frank; it drew her to him. He was strong and assertive. More so now that they won this skirmish. Sam's attitude and demeanor were still a lingering problem, but Frank had the organizational skills of running the herd and the understanding of how to protect the Clevengers in any given Indian attack. John followed Frank's lead. He was used to helping and following men with skill, but had influence on Frank as well. John's military experience with rogue Indians helped Frank and gave him some peace that he would not be alone in these unpredictable attacks. The duo worked well together and each man complimented each other.

The Clevengers, John, and Frank reached the fort and were greeted by several men, including J. Swap, who pointed out where they could put their things and stay for the night. It was late evening and time to turn in.

Chapter 8

A Bit Friendly

The first few weeks at the fort passed quickly. Sam's vote was the only one that counted in the Clevenger democracy. It was his decision to stay longer to recover from the long traveling days and the Indian incident just days before.

John had a local blacksmith shorten the barrel of his Colt. The factory barrel length on his Cavalry Single Action Colt was a nuisance when riding on the wagon's buckboard. The holster had a hole worn clear through from the barrel constantly tapping and rubbing the wooden seat. After the work on the pistol was complete, the blacksmith cut the issued holster and replaced the end with a wood plug.

It was late afternoon into the third week when Frank reached his limit and became restless. "Dammit, Johnson, we'll end up crop farmers fer good if'n we stick around here anymore."

John chuckled. "Yup, only roots grown around here is them outta ol' man Clevenger's backside. I think he's a bit spooked and don't want to see no more Injuns. Swap told me this morning them Navajo have really put the cinch on everyone in these parts. They pushed the Hopi up top the plateaus. Hard times up high like that—not much water and hard to farm too. The peach orchard behind the fort is hid a bit by the valley, but come time for them to ripe, Navajo be sneekin' in and eatin' better than the rest."

Holding a piece of jerky, Frank nodded as his teeth stripped back a piece of sinew while he chewed. Jessie stepped out from under a shade structure close by and called for Frank. "Frank, can you give me a hand? Sam told me to grease the axles on the wagon."

Frank's face grew a large smile. John saw the blushing grin. "Oh boy, I seen that, Frank. You're in for some trouble, I reckon. I ain't your daddy, but you watch yourself hangin' around that girl."

Frank let out a small giggle. "What? Naw man, you don't know what you're talking about." Standing and brushing the dust from his chest and thighs, Frank fixed the brow of his cowboy hat and scampered off behind Jessie. John stood from the water barrel he was sitting on and whispered to himself, "Goin' to grease axles, yep."

Frank explained to Jessie with extreme detail the wheel hub and axle assembly as he cleaned, inspected, and greased the bushings. She crouched in looking as if she was very interested in what he was explaining. But it was the soft, intense tone that drew her attention. Frank felt Jessie's breath on his left ear as she slowly moved closer. Almost finished, Frank lost his concentration on the task momentarily. He tipped his left hand back and turned to face Jessie, placing his thumb and pointer finger on her chin. He rested his right hand on her shoulder just for a second when Sam startled the two, barking, "What the hell? It doesn't take two to grease axles."

Frank rocked back on his heels from his crouch and fell onto his backside. "Sam! You can't be sneekin' up on me like that. Scared all hell outta me."

Jessie laughed with grease smeared across her chin. She stood and turned away quickly. Swap was riding by and noticed the mess of axle grease on Jessie. "Girl, look at ya. You got a bit of a mess there, don't ya?" Jessie started to wipe at her face when Swap finished. "Not yer chin—it's that print on yer shoulder there. I reckon that's a bit big for your hand. Better get that taken care of before yer ma sees it." Jessie nodded with a blush. Swap kicked his horse a bit and rode on to a nearby hitching post and dismounted. John saw Swap chatting from a distance with Jessie and asked him, "Swap, pretty girl, eh?"

Swap answered, "Yep, not many look that perty after traveling across Arizona Territory. She looked a bit flustered there. Must have the sweets for that Willson fellow you're travelin' with." John scratched Swap's horse behind the ear. "Yup, trouble be comin' I say. I figure they may be gettin' a bit friendly."

The time spent at Camp Windy gave Frank, John, and the Clevenger family the needed rest to move on with more confidence. Information from J. Swap was very helpful in that he had made the trip to Camp Windy before and knew some details on how the hostile Indians traveled. Swap had given John and Frank some tips on how to navigate the wagons and guide the herd of cattle and horses off the slope into Lee's Ferry's south crossing. The new trail was newly established to the south crossing, but only usable during a certain time of year. Sand and boulders could make for a long day dropping into the Grand Canyon. This time of year was a good time to cross. A month earlier would have been better, but the water was still low and the daytime temperatures fairly mild with evenings still cool as long as the storm clouds stayed to the horizon. These usually hit hard and fast with no mercy, and were very unpredictable.

~~~~~~~ *Chapter 9* ~~~~~~~

May 5, 1886
Lee's Ferry, Grand Canyon, Arizona Territory

"Sam, do you think it's a good idea to be headin' out of here?" Charlotte asked Sam. "I'm still a bit nervous about the Indians."

"You just relax. It's been plenty of time, and Ol' Swap said they haven't seen any fresh sign for a few days. Don't worry yourself about it. Once we get movin' we can all settle down and forget all that back there."

Today was warmer than usual and the wind had died down some. About four miles north of the fort, Charlotte called to Sam, "Samuel, can we stop for a spell? I don't feel so well and I could use…" "We just got started!" Sam interrupted. "What in hell could you need a rest from? You been sitting in the back of that wagon on them quilts for better part of a week. I reckon that be rest enough." Several weak coughs came out of Charlotte as she inconspicuously dabbed a small amount of blood from her lower lip.

Jessie spoke up. "Ma'am, I see you been bleedin' some from your mouth when you cough. Mr. Clevenger knows you have the lunger disease. He don't say anything cause he thinks you'll be getting better soon. I don't think you'll be getting better soon. Your color ain't good and you look real pale since we left home. You ought to lay down. I'll ride with Frank for a spell and give you some room in here."

Sam overheard Jessie. "Yep. I told you, Charlotte. Those soldiers most likely passed you the TB sickness. I always said nursin' them boys could only come of harm. After feedin' and carin' fer those men I just ain't surprised." Sam was making clear reference to

Charlotte's good nature. She boarded soldiers from time to time and Sam didn't take to it.

Charlotte took a slow sip from an opium elixir bottle as several drips rolled from the corner of her mouth. Jessie wiped the old woman's face and dismounted the wagon to ride with Frank.

It was midmorning and the dew had just lifted from the weeds. Sam rode up to the front of the wagon next to John. "Sam, why are you so damn bent all the time? Seems you don't have a bone in ya that can look to the better nature of things."

"See here, son, I am not a pessimistic man. I am just plain optimistic that the worst will prevail. That there is Sam's law, son."

John shook his head. "Well, Sam's law sure keeps you on the outs with folk. You keep that up, sir, and you're gonna end up shot."

Sam didn't like John's statement. He kicked his horse and spoke back to John as he rode ahead. "Ah hell, no young nigga boy knows about white man's business."

Breakfast was cold biscuits and warmed-up rabbit from dinner the night before. John had found a low point in some foothills with a seep full of sagebrush and healthy cottontail rabbits the previous morning. John snared three large bunnies before late afternoon.

"Johnny, you kinda gotta knack fer that trappin', don't chu?" Frank curiously asked with Jessie sitting close to his side.

"Yeah, my daddy had a gift for it, and he done passed it down to me. It takes a real good eye to get that string hole just the right size and position so as the bunny's feet go under and the head goes right in the loop. Sometimes you catch 'em around the belly anyways. But, I'll tell you what, ifn' we had a couple number three muskrat traps it'd be much easier. You just find a dried-up wash with a bunny hole in the side, bury it up with the flap just dusted with sand. That right there gits 'em every time."

Jessie interjected her opinion. "Frank, I bet you could just shoot two or three just by walking around camp a minute."

"Yeah, but we don't need no noise to be gettin' any Injuns all riled up. They hear a couple shots and sure enough, they'd show up here real quick."

"You just shoot them too. I ain't so afraid. I'll even take that shotgun of Ol' Sam's and kill some myself."

John, Frank, and Jessie sat together and chewed the meat off the bones from the last of their breakfast. John changed the subject. "We gots a big day of downhill to the ferry, I reckon. We should be checkin' our rigs and get ready. It's gonna take us all of a day and some rough downhill to get there."

Lee's Backbone was the old route that was much worse than the newer path the Johnson boys recently cleared, but still quite risky with the herd and equipment. Incidents on the trail were frequent and expected. The sand dune descent was the Clevengers' hard est trial to this point.

*Lee's Backbone and the Colorado River at
Lee's Ferry, Arizona Territory*

John leaned back from the buckboard to calm Charlotte. "Mrs. Clevenger, you just hang on in there. Try to relax. Your wagon is real sturdy and you ain't got nothin' to worry about." The two wagons creaked and popped as the torque from the shifting gear slammed side to side. Mrs. Clevenger shook nervously in the back of the wagon. She faced the rear and looked uphill behind the wagon.

Sam was quite uncomfortable and quite shaken himself. "John, slow the hell down!" he ordered.

John ignored Sam and was doing the best he could to keep the team of horses from running down the slopes. He knew that one inch of slack in the reins would send the team full speed downhill, causing the wagon to bounce vigorously and possibly start to dismantle itself. It would most likely explode into splinters, and a landslide of equipment would hurl down the dune, over the rock ledges nearing the bottom, eventually splashing into the muddy water of the Colorado. John had no fear. He was quite capable of driving a team across bad terrain.

With a sinful smile, Frank rode up next to John and simulated a pushing motion, secretly nodding toward Sam.

John shook his head and laughed. "Yep, I know what you're thinkin'. It'd sure make this trip a whole hell of a lot easier if that old bastard would trip over that edge by pure accident."

The sand dune slowly became a rocky trail as midafternoon passed. Nearing the bottom just above the river, the trail was on such a slope that rocks and boulders regularly fell into the path from the slopes above. Boulders had to be moved with manpower and usually a pick or log for leverage.

Reaching the bottom was quite a relief. Some unexpected dark clouds quickly gathered above. Many dark clouds had been lingering to the north and east. The herd was easily managed as the thirsty animals occupied themselves with the relief of the water.

Frank hollered, "Git out that Starr carbine, John. We gotta alert the ferryman we're here. Don't wanna use my good shells, less I'm shootin' at critters."

John reached out from behind the buckboard of the wagon and strolled up the riverbank with Frank and Jessie. The shot could easily spook the herd, so a couple hundred yards around the bend would be necessary before cracking off a round. "Here, Jessie, do the honors." Frank handed her the short carbine and a paper cartridge from his pocket. She loaded the rifle and pointed it randomly at the ledges to the north side of the river. She fired the shot. Powder and sparks shot back into her face and she immediately dropped the gun to the ground. The shot echoed up the steep walls of the Grand Canyon, along with the clash of the rifle into the rocks at her feet. "What a piece of junk!" Jessie barked.

Frank nervously grabbed her and inspected her face. John looked over Frank's shoulder with concern. "Good thing you chickened out and closed your eyes when you pulled the trigger," John said. "That fire surely would of blinded ya or at least stung for a bit."

Frank pushed John away with his elbow. "Damn it, John, quit yer foolin'. Spooked me a bit too, ya know. I figure this gun had been used for a club before we snagged it up from that Injun. Damn breach is all worn out, loose action and cracked stock to boot."

About then is when Warren Johnson, the ferryman, yelled out from the north bank. "Afternoon, ya'll! I'll be over shortly. Get your herd and wagons ready for crossin'!" All three onlookers waved their hands high and returned to fetch the wagons and herd.

The small, skinny ferryman didn't look like much, but he had a deep voice that could intimidate a bear. When he spoke through his beard, which covered his mouth completely, people noticed. His pants were ragged and short, midway up his calves. This was his ferryman wardrobe. When Warren reached the south bank, Frank grabbed the rope tossed over by Warren and anchored it to a large post on the bank. "Warren Johnson, folks. I'll be doin' this ferry crossin' for ya. I'd like ya'll to give me your full attention and as much able-body help as you can offer. I've been doing this for some years now, but it's still a might bit risky with all this equipment." Sam strutted up in front of the group and firmly shook hands with Warren. "Sam Clevenger. I'm heading this party. Before we get to crossing, I assume you'll be asking for the funds to ferry us across this small trickle of a creek." Sam's negotiating started with his downsizing of the situation. He continued, "I suppose you'd take a couple bags of flour for the small inconvenience of our company?"

Warren laughed at Sam and sternly replied, "Mister, I don't think you know where you are. This is the Mighty Colorado. Many a men stood in the spot you're standing at and soon after lost their lives. Colorado don't care much what you call her, 'cause when you drop toe in her current, she'll roll you up in a broken heap and slam the chunks of your corpse against the rocks all the way to Mexico. You respect the importance and treachery of this place before you start with me. If you plan to talk more 'bout it, I'll just scoot back across and let you think on it for a few days. Water is on the rise this time of year. That dark cloud yonder is 'bout to hit. If it rained up there this mornin' you'd be in the drink right now. I ain't your savior, neither. Ifn' you go arms and legs splashin' down river, its over for ya. So by all means, stand around and think about it."

Sam stepped back and swallowed a gulp of pride. Frank rolled his eyes at Sam, clearly amused at the rehearsed spiel the ferryman had just laid out.

Frank had to speak. "I apologize, Mr. Johnson, for his behavior." Frank handed Warren a palm full of silver dollars and the Star carbine. The ferryman poked the pile of silver, meticulously counting each one. With a wide smile from his skinny face, he accepted the rifle and the money. It was always polite to pay the ferryman before crossing, not that Warren would have it any other way.

The ferryman barked a few orders to John and Frank to block wheels and secure the larger of the two wagons to the ferry before launching.

Soon after launching the ferry with the wagon, while moving slowly across the Colorado, Frank noticed Sam's uncomfortable position against the rear wheel of the wagon. "Sam, you look a bit spooked there. If you white knuckle that wheel spoke any tighter, you're bound to bust it!"

Sam scowled at Frank, but held his firm grip. His nasty frown at Frank was only half because of Frank's comment, but also because Jessie had one arm latched to Frank. Sam knew Jessie was putting on an act that the ferry was something to be feared. He steamed as he slowly watched Frank and Jessie's relationship grow.

"Sam, kick that wheel block back into place!" Warren yelled as the block popped loose and nearly slid off the back of the wagon. Sam tried to stretch back with his right leg and slide the block back into place without having to let go of the spoke. "Damn it!" he hollered.

The ferry was nearing mid-current when the rain started. It poured immediately and without mercy. No sprinkles of warning—just a full-blown downpour.

Sam reached back on a second attempt and, as he lost the grip on his spoke, he fell hard to the wet deck. The pouring rain slammed the ferry deck, then bounced upward, creating a violent slippery water dance. Frank handed Jessie off to John and stomped back to help the old man from sliding into the river. Jessie quickly refused John's hand and promptly found her own grip on a side rail. Sam accepted Frank's help, but only to the point when he was back on his feet. He immediately jerked away and yelled at Frank. "You keep off me, boy!"

Frank let go and started to walk away. The old man just had to speak again as Frank turned around. "Son of a bitch, and you keep hands off my Jessie too!"

Frank spun around without a blink and lunged at Sam with a cocked fist.

John had moved in close enough to grab Frank by the back of his suspenders, pull him back, and cuss at the two angry men. "Come on now, ya'll can finish this later. Let's git off the water alive, you damn badgers."

Sam and Frank shook the fight off for today. Just for today. The chuckwagon still remained on the south side of the river for the second run. Warren, John, and Frank agreed to fetch the chuckwagon. The girls and Mr. Clevenger headed to the Johnson homestead to dry.

Warren approached Frank and John briefly in a mild tone. "I see your employer there has a bit of a swelled-up skull. Ain't many men gots the swingers or the notion to negotiate a crossing fee, being that this here's the only ferry in operation. Another thing, when we gits back across, John, you be careful of mu dog Tyrone. Tyrone's the black curly haired one, like you. He only seen a couple of blacks before and he may git ahold of your leg at the cuff. You jist smack him down a bit—he'll scoot off."

John laughed out loud. "Yes, Mr. Johnson, sir, I'll leave him be. And when I do, I'll be sho to give him his space."

The men loaded the chuckwagon secured to the ferry and began the ferry ride across the river. Luckily, Frank convinced Sam and Warren to leave the herd till morning, as a clear sky and a fresh day would tend to the temperament of the agitated animals. Mules and horses alike would wait out the night on the bank until the next day. Rain and wind made for a docile temperament of the herd as their backsides leaned into the direction of the storm.

The deck of the ferry rocked in the muddy river water as it was quickly rising. The men had loaded the chuckwagon onto the ferry reluctantly during this hard-hitting storm. Johnson assured it was a short-lived storm due to its direction, but this assurance was failing.

"Frank, give that front tie-down a tug! Seems to be loose some!" Warren yelled.

John was on the opposite side doing the same, but his knot was not completed well and fell loose. At the time Frank gave a heaving pull, John lost grip of his rope and the wagon jolted forward. Frank fell to the deck and his legs spun off into the water. He quickly clutched a rail and regained position. With a single heave, his arms and legs kicked and landed him on his belly atop the ferry deck. Water and short waves were topping the deck and making for a slippery surface. Warren was dragging behind the wagon, sliding without traction to hold it from its forward roll. John nearly broke his arms as the wheels turned and folded his limbs fumbling at the wagon wheels. The river rapids grew with the storm's intensity, rocking the ferry uncontrollably side to side. All three men were forced to their knees and they could do nothing to stop the chuckwagon's descent. The front wheels dropped off the deck, while Frank grabbed a rope and lashed it to a rail just in time for Warren to whip out a large knife and cut it. "What the hell!" Frank yelled and didn't know why Warren cut his rope.

Warren yelled to Frank, "You gonna pull the whole ferry down with it. We can't tie it off now—too late for that!"

The force of the water against the front wheels tore the chuckwagon from the deck. As the water crushed the wagon into scrap lumber, all its contents splayed out into the water. Cans, flour, bags of wheat, some items floating, some sinking. The brown water swallowed the parts and it was all gone in seconds.

Regaining traction was now an effort due to the strain the men exerted trying to save the chuckwagon. They pulled themselves back to the safety of shore and returned to the Johnson homestead soaking wet and defeated, but not before Sam lashed out at John and Frank. "You dumb son of a bitches! That chuckwagon had most of the damn provisions for this godforsaken trip! You can bet you muttly looking rat bastards are paying for that! I'm gonna ration you two down to a biscuit a day!"

Sam was all steam. Frank and John knew it would wear off soon. John asked Frank, "Look at ol' wet Clevenger—is that what a Mugwomp looks like?"

"Naw, a Mugwomp is a lazy fat bird. A bird who sits on the fence with his mug on one side and his womp on the other. Ol' Sam there looks more like a Navajo chicken who fell in the outhouse hole."

John laughed. "Crow. You mean a piss-wet crow!"

"Yeah, boy, that's what I mean."

"Quite the menagerie, eh, boys?" Mrs. Johnson said as she dished up the hot stew to the soaked crowd seated at her dinner table.

"Not the first time we lost a wagon in that river. Even on a good day we have lost horses, cattle, and wagons, and even a few unlucky men have perished. Consider yourselves lucky."

"I can give you a hand with that." Mrs. Clevenger offered her hand to help, but Mrs. Johnson refused. "Naw, you just relax. Jessie and I can get his."

The sons of Warren Johnson—Prince and Jeremiah—were also seated at the table, acting in the usual adolescent manner.

"Do you two mind? Why can't you just sit still and eat like normal people do?" Jessie asked the two fidgety boys. She thought them to be much younger because of their immature mannerisms, not knowing they were actually a little older than her. "Knock it off, Jer," Prince yelled at his brother after catching a shin kick under the table.

"What? I didn't do nuthin," Jeremiah lied back to Prince. Warren had just walked in and heard the last of the boys' little tussle. He strolled up behind them and smacked both boys on the back of their heads.

"Frank, quit your giggling," Jessie said, trying not to laugh herself. She continued, "Did shut 'em up quick, didn't it?" John sat quietly and started to eat. He didn't approve of anyone's behavior. Sam, Mrs. Clevenger, John, Frank, and Jessie all had eaten several large bites of stew when Warren sat and started a prayer with his family. The guests never realized the Johnson family was somewhat religious. Feeling a bit ashamed, the guests dropped their heads and allowed Warren his grace, trying to disguise their large mouthfuls.

"Dear kind heavenly father, please bless this food before us today. Please bless the crow and drowned mice that makes this nourishin' stew..." The guests all slowly looked up at each other with disgust as Warren continued, only now with a large, toothy smile: "And Lord, please give us all hope my boys don't continue to make fools of themselves in front of our guests, and especially the young lady Jessie, as these boys may never find a woman willing to show notice to their childlike behavior. I'd like to ask Thee to rise the sun as early as possible to send our visitors on their way. I ask Thee to make me strong and tolerant of their ungodly ways long enough for their departure..."

"Warren," Sam interrupted, "can you get on with it? Damn stew is gettin' cold." Warren continued further without notice to Sam. "Lord, I am especially thankful for the table Mr. Lee left for us outside and the bottled strength to kick these heathens from my home to finish their cold crow stew in the rain, in the name of Jesus Christ, Amen." Only Charlotte, Warren's wife, and his young boys joined in his finished prayer. "Amen."

Mrs. Johnson spoke up. "It's beef stew. Warren likes to mess with folks."

Later that evening, Sam and John stood at the back of the wagon, unloading some bedding for the women. Sam asked John, "Where you sleeping, boy?"

"The lee side of the house will be fine. Looks like this little squal is lettin' up a bit. Warren said storms in these parts hit hard, but roll on out pretty quick. I can see the stars clear up yonder up wind. I reckon it's fine."

"Well hell, I ought to stay out in the wagon with Frank. I can't see them Johnson kids getting to sleep anytime soon. I'm headed for the outhouse."

John left the wagon and carried two bedrolls into the house. Sam double checked that John made it all the way inside before he kneeled down and unhooked the iron pot from the rear of the wagon. He stepped quickly towards the outhouse a fair thirty yards from the house. "Oh!" He tripped up on a sandstone rock overturned by a horse hoof near the front of the outhouse. The iron pot slammed the ground and the lid slid open. The wire held the lid on for the most part, but not enough to hold several of the gold eagles from spilling out. Sam quickly regained his footing and tipped the pot upright.

The dim lantern he carried didn't glow enough for him to see too clearly. He slid his right hand around in the sand, dragging his fingers like a rake, and gathered the few gold pieces that had escaped. The outhouse was directly in front of him, but Sam jogged right past it. He was looking for a secure place to stash the pot for the night away from the wagon. Everything seemed to go smoothly after his mishap. He entered the house looking for John and noticed quickly John wasn't in the house. Just then, John pushed the door open and came in, just following Sam. Sam had no idea John had made it back out to the wagon for another load of blankets.

John asked him, "So what did you find? Saw you on yer knees diggin' around."

"Tripped up—stubbed my toe somethin' fierce."

John had a hard time seeing Sam in the dark, but did manage to notice he was carrying something in both hands. Frank returned from checking on the herd. He would sleep in the wagon that night, normally where Mrs. Clevenger slept, but the Johnsons' home had enough room for the women.

A few hours passed into the night and the homestead fell quiet.

"John. Hey, John," Frank whispered from the wagon while lying on his back. It had to be nearly morning, but John heard him. "Yeah, them coyotes is keepin' me up too," John answered.

Frank popped out of the wagon and walked over to John. They both sat and leaned against the side of the house, whispering. "Hey, John, look at this!" Frank held up a shiny gold coin. The gold glimmer from the moon was quite impressive. The coin was obviously newer and not circulated enough to lose the shiny luster. This was John's first observation. "Where in hell you'd find that?" John asked.

"Just 'for I went to bed I paid a visit to the outhouse—saw it gleamin' in the dirt right there." John now knew it wasn't the coyotes that kept Frank awake. It was his find that kept him stirred up.

John also put two and two together and realized just what had happened.

"Frank, you keep that to yourself. I watched ol' Clevenger trip in the dirt right there. He must have dropped it."

Frank smiled. "Damn! I wonder if that ol sum-bitch has a bunch more of these." John remembered Sam was carrying something other than just a lantern. It was just too dark for him to see what it was.

He was quick to discount anything that might get Frank more excited. "Naw, I bet it just jumped his shirt pocket when he fell. He may be lookin' for it in the mornin'. Go back to bed—get some sleep." Frank returned to the wagon for the remainder of the night, and of course didn't sleep a wink.

Chapter 10

May 16-19, 1886
Jacob's Pool to House Rock Springs

Frank and John were able to fit the whole heard of horses and mules into the corral at Jacob's Pool. Several hungry coyotes had been following the travelers since leaving Lee's Ferry. Frank had become quite irritated with the hungry pack. There was a mare in the herd that was prepared to foal. Frank was determined to protect the newborn from coyotes, for he knew the most vulnerable time for stock to be subject to predators was during birth.

The mare foaled early in the morning before the sun broke the horizon back to the east over the cliffs. The foal found its legs, and the mother did a fair job of protecting her baby. Jessie kept a close eye on the mare after Sam told her the foal would be hers to keep for all the work she had done on the drainage network on the Clevenger ditch back home.

When the sun finally broke, the spooked herd stomped and whinnied nervously in the corral. Coyotes darted in and out of the small arroyos surrounding the Clevengers' camp and corral. The coyotes perched only to have a quick look and make an assessment of their plans. The anxiety and stress finally exploded and the herd began running in a circle wildly in the corral. A large stallion managed to bump and break down the worn juniper post gate. Spooked horses funneled out and scattered quickly to the gullies below the cliffs.

"Shoot them sons o' bitches, John!" Frank yelled as he emerged from the entry of the sod house, frantically trying to get his suspenders buttoned. John, who was cooking breakfast over a campfire, spotted one of the coyotes as it jumped over a gully near the corral. He ran to the wagon, yanked one of the rifles from behind the buckboard, and drew a steady bead just ahead of the varmint. The crack of the rifle startled the few remaining horses. Confused, they ran south into the valley flats. He missed. The bullet zipped under the coyote's chin. After judging the coyote with a second round from the lever action, a third shot found its mark and ripped through the animal's hind quarters. The dog yelped, spun three times, biting at the wound. He soon darted off into a low ravine that would eventually guide him safely to the Grand Canyon.

"Well hell, at least he won't be hangin' round here anymore," John said. "I guess we best be getting the herd back in order."

"Yup, I reckon we got all day to get 'em all back. One more night here ain't gonna kill us, and with your shooting them coyotes we're plenty safe."

"Didn't you see that?" John said, quick to answer. "I hit that song dog square. He won't make it far."

Frank shook his head and laughed as he spoke, "Yeah, whatever, man. That varmint's home free. They tough as hell. I once saw a two-legged coyote, both legs on the same side. He'd hop up, run a bit, then lay back down quick like. Fast as hell and looked quick nuff to catch a rabbit, or a mouse at least."

"You kiddin' me?" John asked.

"Less'n I didn't see if for myself, I would never had believed it neither," Frank replied with a laugh.

Sam strutted out of the house and sternly yelled at John, "Hey, boy, you run out and fetch Jessie. Frank can start gatherin' the herd on his own for now."

Jessie was collecting firewood midway to the spring when the commotion started. A yearling colt ran past her up the canyon path in a mad rush to escape the coyotes. She untied the firewood and dropped it to the ground, keeping the rope to catch the strayed horse. She could hear John yelling for her: "Jessie! Jess!"

After a short hike partway up the trail, John yelled up the red rock canyon again. "Can you hear me?"

Jessie was quickly climbing the trail to the north and was near the spring, ignoring the calls. The cool, clear water leached from the ledges of the Vermillion Cliffs. She could hear John just fine as his echo bounced back and forth from ledge to ledge. John became agitated with her, knowing damn good and well she could hear his call. He continued yelling, "Come on now. I don't want ol' Sam to get feisty and holler at ya! Just come on back!"

Jessie found the colt drinking from a seep, not far from the top of the trail. The short rope was just the right length to loop behind the colt's ears and neck. She started her return to the valley, purposely not answering. Breathing hard, John stopped and glanced up the path. He spotted her leading the horse down toward him and tried to gain her attention again. "Damn, girl, why you gotta be that way? You is a nice young lady and I gots no quarrel wich ya."

Jessie led the colt past John and down the sloped trail without a word. She had gone down the slope enough to reach a turn in the path, out of John's sight, even before he was finished talking. He threw a rock down the slope of the canyon out of frustration.

The sun seemed to rise very slowly the next morning and the travelers were well on their way. Some miles had passed quickly in the flats below the Vermillion Cliffs. A gray film coated the sky, and the horizon held a mild yellow glow through the clouds. "Looks like rain up top there." Frank pointed to the West.

The mountains to the west were steep, and a large, black cloud began forming, capping the ridgeline. They would reach House Rock Spring before day's end.

"Sam!" Jessie yelled to grab Sam's attention from her comfortable seat in the back of the wagon. Sam turned and she continued, "The mare and her baby are fallin' behind again!"

"Damn it, girl, I'm getting' damn tired of them sum-bitches. Frank, git back there and shoot that foal. We ain't gonna be held up this whole damn trip cause that skinny-legged youngin' can't keep up."

Frank sternly answered, "Oh, hell no! You got the wrong man for that."

John intentionally stayed back when Sam abruptly stopped the wagon to scold Frank. "You work for me, boy! I tell you to shoot that horse, you shoot the horse!"

Frank hollered back at Sam, who was riding shotgun on the wagon. "Listen here, you old peckerwood, that there foal is Jessie's. You done gave it to her and you ain't got no right to just kill it, or have'n me kill it!"

Jessie's face was red with fury. She did nothing but stare at Sam. Hatred had taken over and her red scold grew into tears that streamed down her face.

Frank yelled at John, "John, run back there and gather up the mare and her youngin."

John replied quickly, "I'm right on it, Frank." John jumped from the wagon and grabbed his saddled horse that was being led by the wagon. He didn't want to be part of the trouble and quickly fell back retrieving the two horses while Frank and Sam continued arguing. "You listen, and you listen close, Willson. I own this equipment, I own this wagon, and till we get to Washington, you do as I say!"

Frank dismounted his horse and approached the wagon. He grabbed Sam by the chest of his shirt with both hands and yanked him off the wagon. Sam fell violently to the ground, rustling up sand and dust.

Sam went to yell when suddenly John fired his Colt into the air and yelled at the men. "Sam, Frank, you boys best quit this quarrel'n. I ain't one to get in anyone's business, but this here's gotta stop."

Sam coughed and put his hat back on. He staggered to the wagon and reached behind the buckboard scabbard to pull out the Winchester rifle. Quickly engaging the lever and chambering a round, he threw up the barrel. Walking to Frank, he pointed it inches from his face. Frank twitched left just in time as Sam pulled the trigger and the rifle fired. Frank hit the ground with a loud scream. He held both hands over his right ear, grimacing at the pain of the sharp crack and the ringing in his head. The blast had missed Frank's ear by less an inch.

Jessie hollered to Frank and jumped from the back of the wagon, grabbing him to see the damage. After realizing Frank was not hit, she stood and looked to see that the foal behind Frank was staggering and could hardly stand. The young horse then fell as if it had no bones in its limbs. Sam had shot the foal over Frank's shoulder purposely. Jessie ran to the young horse as the blood ran from its shoulder. Charlotte had awaken from inside the wagon and stumbled to Jessie's side. The mare wouldn't let Jessie get close, but it didn't matter. The young horse lifted its head, drooling pink-colored blood from its lips, then released a final breath from its lungs. Everything went silent except for Jessie's weeping and Charlotte's attempt to comfort the heartbroken girl.

The travelers regained the trail and started again. Frank pushed ahead and gathered a few strayed horses from the herd, keeping himself well ahead of the wagon. The next few hours went by without a word spoken.

Dust on the next sandy rise could be seen moving toward the wagon. Two riders emerged over a hill a mile or so ahead. "Must be the Post to be riding without no wagon or supply mules," John said. He recognized the silhouette of two U.S. Mail riders with large saddlebags outstretched and bulky at the rump of the two horses.

The riders approached and introduced themselves. "Sixtus Johnson, U.S. Mail. This here's Zadok Judd. Weez headed to Camp Windy by way of the ferry, then we'll be headin' back up this way." Zadok was a slim, bearded older gentleman. Sixtus was just a young man, about sixteen or so. He looked happy to see people and appeared to invite conversation.

"Afternoon, folks." Zadok tipped his hat in greeting.

John offered a greeting to the two men, but Sam stared quietly ahead without an introduction. Sam's bodily gestures suggested he had no interest in any conversation; he just wanted to move on. The previous incident had not been settled and left him quiet and bitter.

"I met your cowboy with the horses up a mile or so. The mare at the back of the wagon looks as if she foaled recently. She was all bagged up, and making a lot of noise."

Sam looked over at Sixtus and replied quickly, "Had to put the little one down—it was slowin' us up." Sixtus noticed the unfriendly tone Sam held and sarcastically spoke, "You have a wagon, mister. Could have put the little one in the back there and loaded some of your gear on the pack mules."

"You mind your mail and leave us be," Sam said as he grabbed the reins from John and made them crack.

The wagon started forward. John tipped his hat and Sixtus followed with the same departing gesture as he rode on. Looking back he saw Jessie sitting next to Mrs. Clevenger. Jessie held a weak hand up in an attempt to wave politely as Sixtus passed.

House Rock Spring was the next milestone in the trek. The spring held plenty of water where nearly all travelers stopped. Tradition for some was to carve their name, or paint it with axle grease on the stone walls surrounding the spring. Frank had reached the spring a bit sooner and settled the herd at the spring water down in the flat land just below the canyon walls. The water seeped from the rocks and an earthen dam held the water pooled for easy watering.

Frank spent some time in conversation with the local blacksmith, who had a small rock building and a shade that covered the forge. The rest of the group soon arrived.

John found Frank with the blacksmith. The grungy blacksmith was a musclebound monster of a man with lots of hair and only a few teeth. The man was making passes over a horseshoe with a large file. He stopped mid-stroke and interrupted Frank when he saw John coming in their direction. "This nigga boy comin' in a friend of yern?"

Frank waved the question off with a quick "Yup."

The two walked away and held a short conversation about a famed name they had noticed in passing carved in the rock: "John D. Lee."

Jessie caught up to the two and followed behind. They were all avoiding Sam and his wife for the evening.

Chapter 11

May 20, 1886
Buckskin Mountain

"**G**ive her more rein!" Frank shouted to John. The two were struggling to force the wagon over the large boulders. The main trail at the base of the Buckskin Mountain was eroded and rough. The storm that passed a few days earlier had caused some gully washers to expand and deposit large, jagged rocks in the wagon wheel ruts, the worst being where the trail began to wind uphill to the west. Sam, Charlotte, and Jessie stood nearby out of harm's way while the men fought upward.

"Git that cedar log and pry up that other wheel, Sam!" Frank directed Sam for some help. The old man helped some, but not enough. Frank dropped the pry log he was using on the opposite side and helped Sam lift the wheel over the boulder.

John spoke up from the buckboard. "We got 'er, boys! Let's git on up there before it's late! Trees look thick up top. We could lose some of the herd ifn' we ain't careful." John manned the team well and soon the wagon was on its way up the gnarly mountainside.

Two hours of the rugged climb landed the Clevengers on a ridgeline that was somewhat level. The overlook was an outstanding view of the House Rock Valley to the southeast. The flats below were fairly sparse, and the juniper tree line thickened with added pinion pine trees as they gained elevation. Everyone was very tired and it was time for a break.

The loss of the chuckwagon was not an unnoticed burden. They were all hungry. Sam had negotiated a purchase of some food from the Johnsons upon their departure, but it was just a notch better than hard tack rations. House Rock Spring didn't have much of anything for travelers to purchase, but Kanab, Utah, wasn't too far beyond the Buckskin Mountain crossing. With some luck, a few rabbits along the way would make it somewhat easy to endure until Kanab.

Unpacking a few corn biscuits from the wagon, Charlotte noticed a problem. She quietly handed out the biscuits, then pulled Sam aside. With her hands near her mouth, she nervously addressed Sam in a quiet voice. "Sam, umm…the pot is missing."

Sam became instantly stiff. He walked to the back of the wagon and cursed, "You good-fer-nuthin' sum-bitches. Where in hell's my pot!"

John tried to speak, but Frank answered sooner, "Probably lost it near the bottom. Them was some of the worst rocks so far. Why in hell you so bent? It's just a damn pot. Ain't like we don't got another."

Sam scowled at Frank, took a large drink from a canteen, tossed it to the ground, and headed off back down the trail. "You just git to the top and set up camp. I'll go get it, dammit." They finished the short lunch break and headed up the last stretch of the slope.

Sam was unhappy and began kicking his way down the sloped trail. He moved quickly (for an old man) and found the pot with the cover still secured tightly about a quarter mile down the slope. It was just as Frank had described. The pot, still sealed with the wire tied over the top, was tucked behind the boulder that had held the wagon wheel captive earlier that day. The wire bail was bent and disconnected from one side. Sam easily managed a temporary fix. He sat on a rock in relief with his eyes focused for a few minutes on a lizard doing pushups on a rock outcropping. The sun beat down now that it was well into the afternoon. Sam's fine tailored clothing looked well worn now, almost matching the appearance of Frank and John's clothing. The vest he wore was faded, his pants had axle grease stains, and his hat had lost its shape. The sweat rings were large beneath his arms.

A loud, dull *thump* hit the dirt near Sam, then a loud whistle and another *thump*.

Dirt and gravel shot up ten feet below Sam. He squinted and focused on the area of impact. A couple of seconds passed before he heard the fainted blast from a rifle. Then the second blast. He didn't realize what it was until then. Sam rolled off his side and behind some rocks for cover. Knowing the shots were coming from an extreme distance, he peered anxiously for movement. He crawled low to get his footing and start up the hill. The pot was very heavy and was not making the ascent upward easy. Sam stopped for a breath after twenty yards or so when a large rifle slug loudly ripped the pot from his grasp. The pot hit the ground and Sam could clearly see the soft lead splatter mark on his iron pot. Some of the splattered bullet fragments penetrated Sam's right pant leg. Blood oozed out of his calf. It continued to seep out and stained his pants to the size of a silver dollar. "Dammit!" Sam's lungs hurt with every breath as he scampered up the slope.

A strange laugh came from a gully in the valley way below Sam. "Uh, Early Clock, yer luckier 'n a leper-…uh…you know, them small green fellers. Early, you know. Them small green fellers with the gold…yeah, you know, Early, them-ns."

"Shut up, Simple." Early snapped at his mentally challenged companion.

The two men sat in a washed-out, sandy gully, what seemed to be nearly a half mile below Sam. Very slowly, Simple continued talking to his partner. "I ain't seen nobody shoot a big gun like dat before. Hu hu."

Early addressed his slow, deep-spoken companion. "Simple, you n' me's gonna get that Injun. I bet he's booby trappin' the trail up yonder. Ifn' you see his buddies, we best skedaddle. I ain't got nuff of these .50-90s to last all day." Early waved the long, heavy rifle cartridge in front of his friend, loaded the Sharps rifle, and slightly adjusted the ladder sight. Early called him "Simple" for obvious reasons. "Simple, I do believe we done put a spoke in the wheel fer that scared Injun. Let's finish our cups o' Arbuckles and head up there sneaky like."

With his dirty hands constantly scratching and pulling at the button on his shirt, Simple nodded with intense interest, drooling a bit from his toothy smile. The two would have been harmless if it weren't for Early's Sharps rifle. They headed to the foothill through way of a gully for cover. Simple galloped like a horse trying to hold his key ring full of keys from clanking. His future aspirations of being a jailer led him to believe a heavy ring of useless keys on his side was good practice, and he enjoyed the fashion. "When we git close, can I do it with du gun, Early? Hu, kin I, kin I, kin I?"

"Quiet, Simple! We gots to be quiet or you ain't gonna get no beads. You hear me now? None." Simple answered Early in a whisper as they scampered. "Yeah, yeah, OK. Hu, hu. Quiet so I kin get some Injun beads. I like dem beads. I like du blue ones, and the red and green ones, and the…"

"SHHHHHHH, dammit!" Early finally got Simple to quit talking for the time being.

Sam had made an upward climb just off the trail to not expose himself for another chance at a long shot. Fifty yards ahead, he could make out the bench where he left the wagon earlier. His breathing became painful as he collapsed with the pot near some sagebrush for a rest, a rest that was a bit too long.

Early and Simple gained ground on Sam quickly. Without any movement from Sam, the two closed the distance to a short hundred yards or so.

"Do you have any beads?" Simple reluctantly yelled out when he saw some movement from Sam. Early quickly stuffed the butt of the Sharps into Simple's belly, shutting him up quickly. "Damn, Simple, now he knows where we zat! You gots to hobble up that lip of yern if'n you don't wanna be crow bait!"

Sam heard the conversation but couldn't make out what Simple had said. He recognized the English, so he replied, "What in hell are you shootin' at me for?"

Simple quickly yelled again out of turn, "'Cause you got beads!" Early tried to belly Simple with the Sharps again, but Simple had learned from the last gut-buster and backed away quickly. Early yelled back to Sam, "I guess you ain't Injun?"

"Hell no, I ain't no Injun!"

Simple whispered to Early, "So he ain't got no beads then?"

Early ignored Simple and yelled back to Sam, "We're sorry, mister! You ain't sour on us, are ya? We'z just headed to Kanab!

Name's Early. I gotta simple man travelin' with me and we ain't shootin' no more!"

Sam was relieved. The two men walked in closer to Sam as he spoke to them. "If'n you boys give me a ride to the top of this ridge, I'll let this one slide. Do you make a habit of shootin' at folks before knowing who they are?"

Early and Simple looked at each other and dropped their heads. They accepted the proposal and returned to the flats, where they had left their horses. They returned and helped Sam up the mountain ridge and met up with the wagon at the end of the day.

Mrs. Clevenger stumbled out of the wagon at the campsite Frank had decided upon. Her words came after several weak coughs. "Frank, do you mind fetchin' me some water?" She leaned in and used Frank's shoulder for support. Frank was visibly bothered by the sickly old woman.

He answered her as he tipped a small canteen into the blue steel mug. "Ma'am, with this cough you been carryin', seems you's ain't getting much better, and a bit blue in the face. You ought not be moseyin' around too much. You're liable to tip over, maybe bust a leg or sumpthin."

She answered back softly, "Yup, with any luck you can bury me in Utah. Washington seems further away every day. I didn't expect my health to expire so quickly once we hit the trail."

Frank sensed the old woman was giving up. Jessie handled all of Mrs. Clevenger's petty requests, and allowed Charlotte to rest in the wagon for most of the trip. The campsite was the first flat area large enough to set up a camp. The juniper trees and sagebrush were quite thick and helped keep the wind to a minimum. John set up the Clevengers' tent and gathered wood for the fire. The rock fire pit was centered in an opening where many people along the trail had camped. This fire pit was one of several positioned furthest to the north of the trail. On this night, it was John's duty to take a head count of the herd. The long, steep hillside left several young horses and mules tired and stranded on the slopes. The retrieval would be easy, as the animals had waited and rested together in a short gully, shaded by a grove of junipers. Frank made certain Jessie and Mrs. Clevenger remained content and comfortable before he left to gather firewood.

Around that time, Early, Simple, and Sam topped the high hillside and, through the thick juniper trees, could see the camp. "Much obliged for the ride," he told Early. "I'll be on my way. You boys just keep movin' on. I don't need your mind-simple friend causin' any trouble at our camp." Sam's instructions came as a bit of a surprise to the two tired men.

Early looked down at Sam from his tired mare. "You know, we'd just be staying next to ya'll and be gone by first light."

Sam abruptly cut him off. "Nope. You boys just ride on. Your poor judgment today nearly killed me, and I can't be havin' your kind too close for too long. With him, somethin's bound to go wrong." Simple never said a word, and his nervous fidgets were very noticeable. Sam intimidated him, causing him much discomfort. Simple picked feverishly at the threads where the shirt buttons were once attached. He and Early rode on down the trail toward the next significant campsite and water hole, Navajo Wells.

Sam scurried into the trees, making certain Simple and Early were out of sight. He quickly found a midsized juniper tree with the limbs drooped to the ground. The shaded canopy left an excellent area under the tree. An excellent place to bury the pot.

"AHH! Dammit!" Sam jumped, fell backwards, dropped to his side, and buried his elbow into the sand.

A large western diamondback rattlesnake slithered in front of Sam as he knelt down to crawl under the tree. The snake disappeared into the brush, hurrying to escape the old man's presence. Gathering his thoughts and crawling forward landed him in a tight opening. There was just enough room to sit up and dig a shallow hole. Sam buried the pot with about two inches of sand covering the lid. The filled hole was just deep enough to conceal the loop handle at the top of the lid. He smiled, patted the dirt, scattered small branches about, and emerged from under the tree. Using a dead limb of sagebrush, he wiped the sand of all tracks he had made up to about twenty feet of the tree.

Sam was just entering the camp when Frank emerged from the west. The large armload of firewood clattered loudly as Frank dropped it near the rock fire pit.

Jessie was peeling potatoes when she saw Sam return to camp. "Samuel, where's the pot?"

"Never mind, girl. You just keep hushed." Jessie rolled her eyes as she turned away. Sam reached out and grabbed her shoulder and, with an open hand, slapped the side of her head. Frank, without hesitation, rushed over and kicked Sam in the small of his back. He fell hard to the sand. The force of the blow took Sam by complete surprise, and the mouthful of brush cut his lips.

Sam grumbled as he spit and stood. "You get the hell outta here, boy! She ain't yours, dammit! I'll fill your belly with buckshot! You son of a bitch!"

Frank started for Sam again, when out of the trees, John rode up through the camp and grabbed Frank by his suspenders and pulled him back. Jessie, still on one knee, regained balance and went back to her business of preparing the meal.

"Damn it, Frank, you gotta calm the hell down!" Frank jerked himself free from John's grasp and pushed the horse away as he walked off into the trees.

Charlotte spoke up from within her tent. "Sam, come on in here and have a rest. It's been a long day so far and you ought to have a rest before we eat."

Jessie waited for Sam to enter the tent with Mrs. Clevenger before she slipped off after Frank. John had left the camp after the scuffle and was already out of sight.

"Frank?" Jessie asked, looking into the trees for Frank. He heard Jessie and walked back to meet her.

Frank was clearly still steaming. "I 'bout had enough of that old bastard, Jessie. I ain't never seen anyone treat a woman so."

"Frank, we should just get outta here right now. We could ride on and John can stay and deal with Sam and Charlotte."

"They'd come after us, Jessie. Sam would have the law after us right or wrong once we get to Kanab. What the hell do you think it would look like? If'n we just up and left, they'd get to Kanab and send a posse to find me. It'd look just like I nabbed you. John's just a half-nigger boy—they wouldn't listen to anything he gots to say neither."

Jessie looked to the ground and then looked up with a change in her eyes. "I hate those damn Clevengers. I always have. They both push me around like a ranch hand. Since my family was killed I guess they got lucky with me. Mrs. Charlotte just ignores everything that old man does. You saw, you saw her back there. She just hides when he gets all mad and violent."

Frank was listening. His hand coursed across his mouth and mustache. He stepped closer to Jessie, looking into her eyes. He pet the side of her head, combing her hair with his fingers. Jessie closed her eyes as she relaxed for a moment. Frank spoke up. "All right then. All right then, Jessie. Their's is coming. I 'bout had enough too." He passed her by and walked back to the camp.

"What's that supposed to mean, Frank?"

Frank lent no reply as he continued through the trees. Sam, just realizing Jessie's absence, shouted for her to return. She sulked back to camp and continued preparing dinner.

John returned from his task of gathering the herd. He dismounted his horse and wrapped a rein over a branch.

Frank pulled a large flint rock, a curled steel that fit his fist nicely, and a burned can that held his char cloth from a leather possibles bag on his saddle. He tore some juniper bark from a tree, folded it in half, and twisted it together. The dry bark shredded and turned to a fine rustled bird nest perfect for his fire. He leaned down, tucked the char cloth deep into the nest, and struck the flint with his steel. One quick strike and a spark ignited the cloth to a red glow that spread across the cloth. Frank tucked the shredded bark into the ember and blew a steady stream of air into the smoking nest. It was only seconds and the bark nest ignited into a large flame. He set down the nest and stacked some limbs and brush over the flames.

The embers of the juniper and sage fire flurried upward as the halved sun started to sit down to the west.

The next morning, John awakened Frank. "Hey, Frank, what do ya say you and me slip down the hill and shoot us a sage hen? I seen a small bunch feedin' 'bout quarter mile down the hill. They didn't seem bothered much."

Frank grabbed the Winchester carbine from the wagon and levered a round into the chamber. He gently thumbed the hammer out of the cocked position. John drew his Colt and followed.

"Let's get on it then. That'd beat hell outta just spuds and beans again."

Frank pulled on his boots and snuck over to the tent. He poked his head in and whispered, "Hey, Jessie, you wanna tag along? We're gonna slip out and find us a sage hen, or a rabbit."

"Yeah, I'm comin'." Jessie was quick to answer and quickly tiptoed around Sam and Charlotte, who were in a deep, early morning sleep.

Upon their return to camp, Frank yelled, "Sam! Hey, Sam! Look here what your girl got us. She's a heck of a shot." Frank held up a cottontail rabbit with a clean head shot.

Sam was sitting on a stump with his back to Frank, John, and Jessie. He never looked up from the fire when he yelled at Jessie. "Listen you! Huntin' ain't no place for a woman. You git yer skinny backside back over here now and make some breakfast!"

Frank turned quietly to John. "Step back, John. This ends today."

John shook his finger at Frank as he walked into the trees. "I done told you, Frank. You watch what you say. You is gonna get in a heap of trouble, maybe even fired and sent on your way."

Jessie replied to Sam while John and Frank were talking, "What mess, sir? I just put that pot of potatoes on the coals to cook before we left. We have a good quarter hour before that breakfast is even worth checkin' on." Jessie hardly finished speaking when Sam thrust his left boot up and kicked the pot of potatoes into the dirt. "How's that for checkin' if it's done. Damn kid."

Frank watched in awe as Jessie knelt in the sand to retrieve the pot, now only half as full of food. Jessie's anger was like a silent scream for help as she looked up at Frank from the deep corners of her eyes.

Sam continued with Jessie. "I watched you cut them damn potatoes last night. Damn things are too big—gonna take an hour to cook through. If I see you talking to Frank anymore I'm sending him off and you can run the herd with John."

Sam kicked Jessie in the side with the bottom of his boot. She fell to her side, burning the palm of her hand on a fire pit rock as she caught her fall.

"Samuel Clevenger, what the hell is wrong with you? I just can't get it right, can I?" Jessie yelled. The tears welled up in her eyes and soon burst out, pouring down her face.

Frank walked quickly to the stump behind Sam that was surrounded with kindling and pulled a stuck hatchet from the wood. The rising sun shined horizontal rays through the trees. Flames flickered in the whites of Frank's bloodshot eyes. He stood directly behind Sam. Holding the Winchester in one hand, he raised the hatchet with the other high above his head. "You've lived long enough, you damned old son of a bitch!"

With a swift and merciless blow, Frank buried the full blade of the hatchet deep into Sam's skull. Sam's body jolted into a stiff, upright position. His mouth opened with a cough and his eyes filled with blood. Jessie screamed out loud, wiped at her face to clear off some of the blood spatter, and jumped away from the fire pit. Frank released the grip on the hatchet, and Sam's body slowly folded headfirst into the fire, hatchet still embedded deep.

John raced over and started dragging Sam's body out of the fire toward the tent.

Charlotte looked out from the fly door of the tent, frightened by Jessie's scream. Jessie ran several yards into the trees and crumbled to the ground, turning and looking back at the camp from her hands and knees. Seeing Sam's body fall and being drug by John, Charlotte gasped and retreated to the tent, falling to her knees. The hatchet was still embedded in Sam's skull, and the horrific scene sent Charlotte into shock. She scrambled to regain her footing and reached for a shotgun that Sam had on the floor of the tent near the back.

Frank yelled, "Don't do it, Charlotte. Damn it, just leave it be." Frank ran towards the wagon to grab his rifle.

Charlotte picked up the heavy shotgun from inside the tent, but struggled and could not get either of the hammers cocked. The old woman yelled out a desperate cry, "Jessie!"

Charlotte was now backed up against the rear inside of the tent in deep shock, feeble and weak. John ran into the tent. He unsheathed his Colt revolver and knocked the shotgun from Charlotte's hand. With a very high arm, he held the Colt by the barrel and swung the butt of the pistol into Charlotte's forehead. The walnut grips of the Colt cracked. She gasped for air as blood streamed from her nose and mouth, rolled her eyes to the sky, and toppled backwards into the tent floor bedding. The blood poured out of Charlotte's ears and nose. Her eyes dilated, twitched, and froze half crossed as if looking out of the tent as her last breath gurgled free.

"Damn it, Frank, now we in a heap of trouble! Just like I said!" John continued in a whisper, "I knew this was gonna get bad."

"I had it taken care of, John! You didn't need to do that!"

Frank then rushed to Jessie, who had started to run off but returned with confusion and horror. "Come on now, Jessie. It's all over, girl. Look at me—come on now. It's all gonna be better now."

Jessie looked away from Frank as he held her shoulders, trying for a response.

The blood-soaked rocks of the fire pit sizzled as the fire continued to blaze. Frank let go of Jessie when he noticed Sam's body lying in the sand near the tent with the hatchet handle pointed vertical. John and Frank both grabbed the body of Sam and drug him into some sagebrush, out of sight for the time being. The two men both kicked sand into the campfire, smothering the remaining flames. The smell of burnt hair and flesh still lingered. Jessie did not watch. She sat down on the ground in shock with her arms folded trying to make sense of what had just happened. "What now, Frank?" she said with a shaking voice.

"I suppose we got a bit of cleanup. Help me get a grave dug, John."

John replied with frustration, "Frank, I got half a mind to just leave you here to deal with it on ya own."

"Oh hell, get over here and gimmie a hand. We gotta get 'em buried. Who knows how many folks will be comin' this way soon."

John retrieved the shovel from the wagon and started to dig. With the dry, rocky sand stiff and cemented, the two graves would have to be shallow. Jessie didn't help with the graves. She climbed into the wagon and adjusted the bedding for some rest. Sam was gone, Charlotte was gone, and the relief was just as intense as the horror and brutality of what had just happened. She felt an odd, unexpected sense of peace.

The graves were dug by both men while Jessie watched. Before the bodies were drug into the damp sand graves, Frank began rustling through the pockets of the burned clothes of Sam.

"What are you doin'?" John asked.

"Remember the gold piece I found? I reckon Sam's got more somewhere. Jessie told me he sold some drainage ditch and water to that Collins fella. I'll find that money, and when I do, this will all just be like a bad dream and go away with some whiskey and time."

John chimed in again with curiosity and a little enthusiasm. "Check in his vest."

Frank did, and hit a jackpot. "Ah nice, here we go. Looks to be about close to five hundred dollars, but no coins." Frank fished through the cash and handed John what he figured was half.

The bodies were in the grave with Sam's body face up and head pointed north. Charlotte was in the opposite direction on top of Sam. John kicked at the hatchet handle until it was freed from Sam's skull, then nudged it into the grave with his foot. The men covered the bodies. They started a small fire on top of the grave to burn the bloody bedding and in an attempt to mimic a campfire. This was also in hopes to mask any odors that were sure to come. The remainder of the day was spent staring at the campfire and preparing for their departure the next day.

"I guess ain't no harm sleepin' in the tent, hu, Frank?"

"Nope, ain't no one else gonna be in there."

John placed his Colt on a short stub of sage brush under a tree close to the tent. He walked a few steps under the juniper limbs and extinguished the lantern's flame that was hanging by its bail.

He kicked off his boots, pulled the canvas door of the tent open, ducked inside and retired early for the remainder of the night. Frank was not so content on sleeping right away. He took a pale of water and sat on the stump near the fire. After covering some blood with a push of his boot, he peeled off his sweaty shirt to wash up. Jessie could see Frank from the back of the wagon. The fire had died to mostly just coals and a small flame. She watched as Frank used a rag to clean his chest and arms.

"Are you going to try and sleep some?" She startled him.

"Pardon me, I thought you was sleepin'." Frank quickly started to put his shirt back on, somewhat embarrassed.

"I don't mind, Frank. And earlier, with Sam and Charlotte, what you did was a good thing. Well, not good, but things will be better now. As bad as it seems, I can handle things."

"Listen, Jessie, ain't nuthin' good about it. We got lots to do now to keep quiet 'bout all this. Seems to be trouble wherever in hell I am. I can't tell if it follows me, or if it's waitin' for me when I get there. You go on back in there and get some shuteye."

Jessie looked directly at Frank with a devious half smile. She unbuttoned the top few buttons from her dress. "You know, the wagon has plenty of room in here for the both of us, Frank."

The morning came quickly. Frank was shaken awake by John whispering. "Frank, sneak on outta there. We got some lookin' to do. I ain't slept but a wink."

Jessie was sleeping with her head on Frank's chest. Both had their clothes scattered about and were buried in blankets. Frank slowly squirmed out of the wagon without waking Jessie. The two men scampered wildly around the campsite, looking for Sam's stash of gold. Digging in everything from the horse tack to the axle grease box, they found nothing.

After giving up a feeble and rushed search, Jessie, Frank, and John continued to Navajo Wells.

Chapter 12

May 22, 1886
Kanab, Utah Territory

The Utah border was thick with sagebrush that the junipers thinned. Jackrabbits and cottontail rabbits where thick and seemed to jump from every other bush as the wagon rattled by. The wind had picked up due to the lack of trees. Navajo Wells was less than a day's ride, as long as it didn't rain. The red silt and blue clay of the area was hell on wagon wheels, and floodwater could prove to be quite the nuisance.

"Whoa, boys!" John pulled stiff on the reins to halt the team of mules. The wagon creaked and popped as usual, then abruptly stopped. Frank rode forward past the herd of horses to see why John stopped.

"What's the trouble? Ya'll good?" Frank muttered.

With a concerned look and a nervous tone, John spoke up. "I can see some riders catchin' ground 'hind us. Jist back there quarter mile or so. Look a bit like them Postal boys we ran into down there before House Rock. I can see that skinny feller with the funny name, Zadok. Yip. Have a look there, Frank. Just coming down that hill there." John pointed, then dismounted the wagon with a step down and a short leap. He dipped a ladle of water from the barrel strapped to the wagon side and took a drink.

"Ah, hell." Frank leaned around and yelled to Jessie, who was riding close behind. "Hey, Jessie, keep quiet. I'll do the talkin'. Ain't gonna be much of it neither. Too much talkin' gonna git us in a heap o' trouble. It's best just keepin' it short."

"OK," Jessie calmly replied.

"But if they start askin' questions, you just smile and be calm 'bout it."

"Yeah, OK, I got it." Jessie was a little irritated at Frank's persistence, as he already seemed nervous.

"Hello there!" Sixtus, Zadok's teenage partner, hollered out while he waved. "Ya'll look a bit ragged. Everything OK?"

"We gittin' along OK," Frank answered fast.

"I see yer mare has finally calmed a bit since last time I seen ya'll. Before I head on past you to Kanab, do ya'll need a Post back to Arizona? You know, let yer kin know you made Utah line? We'll be headin' south again in a week's time." Zadok was talking directly to Frank.

"No, sir. No kin to speak of back there."

"Where's the ol' man and his wife? They back there in the wagon?" Zadok became curious.

"No, sir, just us. Me and him and Jessie."

Frank's eyes glared at Zadok and Sixtus. His mind raced as his options deteriorated.

Frank thought to himself: I'm gonna have to shut these two up. Being Postal delivery men they surely know everybody in these parts. They talk a whole lot and ask too many damn questions.

Frank continued to answer the men between his thoughts. "Ol' man and his wife headed off the north fork before we topped off on to Buckskin. They's headin' for Paria." Frank second guessed his words. John didn't think this was a clever response either. Frank knew this by the way John dipped his eyes to the ground to hide the shame of the strange answer. Who in their right mind would take their sick wife and put her on a horse to ride to Paria?

John spoke up as another thought crossed his mind. "Nail's Best, boys! We got word a shipment reached Paria when we was down House Rock way. Ol' Sam be hankerin' for some of that local wine."

Frank looked at John trying to figure out what the hell he was talking about.

"Oh yes!" Sixtus replied. "That's some good news! Injuns took quite a likin' to Nail's and been darn lucky in stealin' a few wagon loads trying to make it this far. Ol' Zadok here makes some good wine too." Sixtus chuckled and continued laughing with a story.

"Back when I was a youngin' me and Naegle got snookered up real good one evenin'. Ol' Naegle got to chuckin' up vittles, grits, and venison. I seen him gittin that ol' rooster neck goin' and heavin' real hard and 'course I had to join right in 'cause I was unsettled myself just from watchin' him. His ol' lady came out a yellin' and..."

"All right then, Sixtus, we gotta get moving." Zadok was not ready to hear the story as it was clearly well rehearsed and he had probably already heard it several times. Jessie giggled a little for the first time since the incident. John and Frank didn't have the mind-set to see any humor.

"Yup. You Postal boys gotta keep on the move." Frank tried to hurry them up by encouraging them to move on. John remounted the wagon and shook the reins. The mules responded and burst into a quick walk.

Frank, John, and Jessie's appearance would make one think they hadn't slept in weeks. The trip to Navajo Wells was uneventful after the meeting with the Postal men. The small herd of horses had a short sip at the water hole and were ready to move on. The weather was cooperating and there was no reason to slow down. The minds of the travelers were completely occupied with gaining distance from the shallow graves still only several miles back. They spoke of ideas, ways, and means of escaping this incident. Talk of splitting or selling the herd and gear, or traveling together and keeping everything until reaching a later town on the trip north, were options on their minds.

With the Clevenger herd pastured at the southeast edge of town, the three weary travelers stopped at the general store with a tired gait in the town of Kanab. Nestled at the base of red cliffs at the mouth of a canyon, Kanab appeared quite serene. The town had adequate water with the green trees, fields, and gardens. The spring green was quite a site. The irrigation water coming from Kanab Creek made this place what it was.

A man leaving the store with a young boy opened the door just as Jessie was about to enter.

Startled, the man spoke up. "Excuse me, ma'am. I apologize. We nearly ran you over! Say, you ain't from 'round here, are ya?"

Jessie replied softly, "No, sir. Just passing through."

"Name's Dobson, Will Dobson. This here's mu boy, Will. Will Dobson."

Jessie snickered as she knelt down to the boy's level. "Well isn't that funny. How do people keep you 'part, seein's how you have the same name?"

The little boy, no more than three years of age, acted as if he didn't hear Jessie's voice. His eyes were fixed over Jessie's right shoulder. The boy was nervously staring at John, who was tending the wagon. John did not notice the boy's gaze.

"Ma'am." The boy spoke, still staring and now pointing, "Papa, see?"

The father pushed his boy's finger down gently, apologizing again. "So sorry, ma'am. Little Will here is a curious little rabbit. You and your husband there (nodding toward Frank) gots the first Negro we ever seen here. We'll be gittin' along now. G'day."

Frank noticed the nod from Will and asked, "Afternoon, sir. Any idea which way to get west from here? I'd go north up the canyon if the road's in shape enough to travel quick."

Will answered, "You best take the canyon as you say. Feller named Nephi got's one hell of a settlement up Zion Canyon, but you do have the option of the Arizona Territory and Utah border out to Winsor Castle way. If'n yer headed to St. George, that is."

"Well, all right then. Thank ya, sir." Frank politely let the man and his boy pass into the street. The boy, still staring at John, nearly twisted his neck as they moved on. Frank and Jessie mounted their horses and John climbed to his buckboard. He could feel the eyes of the town inspecting his every move. John was becoming increasingly unsettled. He had spent his time in the military surrounded by black soldiers with white superiors, so the racial tensions were minimal compared to what he felt in Kanab, in that everyone and everything appeared so white. White folks were everywhere. With the heavier military presence in Southern Arizona and Texas, there was a mix of some Indian, Mexican, and black folks all intertwined into society. This was John's first experience with a Utah town, and he was a little shocked to say the least. It was clear by the demeanor of passersby on this street that it was uncommon, and maybe not so welcome, to have a black man passing through town with a white cowboy and a young woman.

Chapter 13

Toquerville, Utah Territory

rank noticed a man emerging from a large rock building's rear doors. "Mister!" Frank called out. "Hey, mister. You John Naegle? That there's yer winery. Ain't it? I been hearin' 'bout it. That there buildin' is a big sum-bitch! I bet ya could fit a whole damn wagon and team in there. How 'bouts I trade you a mule for a couple cases of yer Nail's Best?"

A wagon clearly could fit in the building for loading shipments of the famed wine known throughout Southern Utah. The giant building had many windows on the first and second floors. The response was met with a laugh. "Who's yer pa, son?" Frank was shocked a bit, as nobody had ever asked that during an introduction. Not sure how to respond, he mumbled out, "Umm, Frank Sr. I guess. Why do you ask?"

Naegle explained with a smile and a little chuckle. "Well, you ain't from 'round here then, brother. I kin tell from yer talkin'. Round here that's how we keep track who's who. I'm bit older n' you, so I'd be closer to knowin' yer pa than you. Call me an Injun, but I be judgin' my wine and brandy dealin' by what I think o' yer kin. You don't have to like that 'bout me, but I *am* the one with the wine. Since you's from outta town, you may not git quite the deal as a local, but I am in need of a mule or two so you're in luck, I recon. Let's have a look at your stock."

One of John Naegle's wives, Mary Louisa, quickly caught Jessie's attention, and the two women introduced themselves. They soon shuffled off together, heading to the upstairs of the winery. The winery was also home to the large Naegle family. Frank commented as they left the entry of the winery, "I guess they got lady talkin' to do."

The wine dealing with Naegle drew some attention from the street. Two men who looked to be in their mid-thirties approached

Frank as he loaded his wagon with newly acquired wine. One of the men asked Frank, "You got more stock you'd be willin' to part with? We can pay cash." Frank's eyes lit up a bit as he replied, "I sure do. Follow me down yonder and I'll show you what we got." Frank led the two men to the small trickling creek downhill to the west of the winery where the animals laid scattered beneath a grove of cottonwood trees. The afternoon sun and cool grass had calmed the herd.

Frank called to John to meet the men. "John, these two men have cash and are looking to buy up our horses." After a short private deliberation between the two men and much finger pointing at the herd, they approached Frank and John with a fist full of cash and a handshake. Frank finished the conversation—"Much obliged, gentlemen. You won't find a better herd of hearty equine."—as he and John headed back up the slope to their wagon.

John was shaking his head and looking only at the ground. He appeared ashamed. "Frank, what in hell are you doin', son? Them ain't our stock."

Frank snapped at John as he divided up the money and stuffed John's left pants pocket with money. "Listen, ol' Sam ain't got any use for 'em anymore. He's busy taking a dirt nap and I sure as hell ain't driven 'em past a town with folks who got cash. You be still about it. We both are in this deep already, together."

John nodded and softly replied, "I rekon so."

With cash in their pockets, John, Frank, and Jessie left the town of Toquerville and rode north. They set up camp halfway between Belleview and New Harmony for the night. Happy, but a little paranoid, they established camp a good distance from the road to not attract travelers for conversation.

John whittled a stick into a stake, then carved a notch at the top. He whittled another stick, a bit shorter with an opposing notch. He tied some sinew snare string to a limb of brush. At the other end of the sinew, he tied the shorter stick. He made a slip knot in another piece of sinew for a snare loop and tied this to the small stick. John used a palm-sized rock to pound in the notched stake, then connected the two notched sticks together. The brush limb was now bowed down to the ground with enough force to hang a rabbit when the notches were tripped. He finalized his setup by enhancing the bunny path by clearing the way through the snare loop. Satisfied with the presentation, John smashed some juniper berries together and dropped them around the trap for a cover scent.

Night fell and the three sat eating some stew John had prepared over the small fire. The snares John had set while Frank and Jessie set up camp rendered a cottontail just at sunset. His craft for catching small game had proven extremely useful.

Jessie sat close to Frank and spoke to John for what seemed like the first time since the Buckskin incident. "John, you got a way about catchin' critters."

John nodded. "Yes, ma'am."

Jessie continued, "You show me how to noose up a rabbit and I'll show you how to clean and cook it. I'm gittin' kinda sick of eating furry stew."

John reached over and took Jessie's bowl out of her hands. With a quick flip, he dumped the stew onto the fire. "There you go, ma'am, problem solved. I be makin' my stew the way I like it. You make your stew the way you like it."

Frank jumped in. "Hey! Come on there, John, why you gotta go and be that way?" Frank gave Jessie his bowl to finish. She smiled at him with a big grin.

John turned his head away. "Ah, please." He then dumped the rest of his stew in the fire and said, "Now that just makes me sick right there—I can't even finish. Ya'll just googlin' eyes over each other."

Jessie laughed at John. The tension around the fire soon drifted.

Frank asked Jessie, "So what did the Naegle lady have to allow? Hope you kept quite 'bout where we came from and whatnot."

Jessie's face lit up as she clearly recalled something funny. "Mrs. Naegle said they seen two crazies last week. She said the smarter one bought some wine and the dumb one had a real bad runny nose. Must have been the cottonwoods, she said. The dumb one only had one button on his shirt. It looked a bit like he picked them all off the way he fidgeted about. He also stirred a small pouch of beads with one finger, peering into it like there was something missing, or a treasure hidden inside."

John laughed out loud. "Ha! That's them two boys that was shootin' at Sam on the Buckskin."

Jessie continued with what Mrs. Naegle said. "She said that too! She said the smarter of the two men said they came from Kanab, same as us. Said they was kinda in a hurry to make it a ways north 'cause they'd done got an ol' man and his family all riled up by mistakin' him for an Injun."

The morning dew dripped off a juniper tree onto John's cheek. He woke slowly with a stretch and proceeded to roll his pack. Frank and Jessie were in the wagon still sleeping. These had been the sleeping arrangements since the night of the Clevenger incident.

"Time to get on it," Frank said. "We gotta make some ground today. I be figurin' on Nevada, John, maybe try to stake a claim. Seems the thing to do ifn' you wanna git away from folks." Frank's traveling plans were a bit ambitious.

"OK then. You sure you ain't gonna take Jessie up Utah way? Maybe even further north? More work and bigger crowd up Salt Lake City way."

"Maybe I'll change my mind by midday. Hell, I don't know." Frank laughed as he packed his bedroll.

Chapter 14

Coyotes and Cadavers

A small group of travelers finally managed to fight the Buckskin Mountain hill where Sam, Charlotte, Jessie, Frank, and John had climbed just weeks before. This hill was a milestone for anyone traveling into Utah from Arizona. The rocky ascent to the top of Buckskin Mountain was the last real tough leg of the trail before Kanab. The potential of losing spokes, axles, and mule or horse legs was very high due to the loose rubble and drainages that could stop a wagon train cold. Once topped off, travelers were greeted with excellent flat camping spots only about seven miles from the Utah border. The thick juniper trees held refuge from the elements atop the Buckskin Mountain grade. This particular time of year could be quite warm in the afternoon hours and quite cold during the night.

"Woe, OK. OK then. What have we here?" The man leading the travelers dismounted and started investigating what looked like a messy abandoned campsite: several empty cans strung about, a sheet blowing in the wind that was hooked upon some sagebrush, a lantern still hanging in a low tree branch.

"Oh, hell. Someone left here in a hurry," he shouted. He quickly turned back to the lead wagon with a middle-aged woman on the buckboard.

"Sorry, ma'am. We have to move on. We will be making Navajo Wells, and maybe even Kanab tonight instead. I apologize for the rush, but there's something happened here from what I just seen in the sand over yonder." The man adjusted his small, round glasses and looked back to what he saw, almost in disbelief.

"Well, what is it?" the woman said.

"I'd rather not say, but I will anyway. There be the hand of a fellow, or a lady, poorly buried shallow and stickin' out of the dirt yonder. Some coyotes been digging around too." The man's voice was shaken as the travelers moved on. The questions were quickly answered from the followers as they all agreed without protest to move on to Kanab to report the findings.

With no time wasted, the group watered at Navajo Wells and continued to Kanab. The man who led the travelers asked whom he should speak to in regards to a possible Indian murder and his findings of a body on Buckskin Mountain. He was pointed to the way of the local judge, Zadock Judd.

"Nice to meet you folks," Zadock greeted. "Could you please give me some of the details? Names, location, what you saw—anything will help." Zadock's introduction was short and to the point.

The man answered, "Sure. I don't know much except we topped the Buckskin and was doin' a quick locate of a campsite when I saw a few things strung about. Things you just wouldn't leave behind. Then I saw a hand stickin' outta the ground. I could see where the coyotes had dug around it some and got to chewin' on it a bit. I didn't stay after that. I got us here as quick as I could to report to the law. Are you the law 'round here? I thought it may be Injuns, but I ain't never heard of no Injuns buryin' no white man. They'd just leave 'em be. And if some white folks came through and buried em, they surely would have said somethin' bout it when they reached Kanab, like you folks."

Zadock replied, "Naw, that Buckskin hill is still in Arizona Territory. Still around five miles or so south of the Utah line. I'll send a telegraph to Prescott. That'd be Sheriff Mulvenon's jurisdiction, Yavapai County. Poor fellow, that be a real pain for him travelin' clear up this way. He's a workhorse of a man, though. I don't 'spect he'll take long to come have a look-see. We'll go up and see what we find so as the coyotes don't eat up the bodies before we can get them named and their kin notified. If'n you'd be kind enough, I'd like you to come along to show me where I can find this camp."

Zadock loaded a horse with some essentials, and a few other men did the same for witnesses and investigation help. The men woke early and headed to the site before daybreak. Upon arrival, two coyotes scampered into the brush as the horse came through the trees to investigate the scene. The hand was still hooked out of the sand and the skin badly torn and chewed with only a couple fingers partially remaining. The men dismounted and slowly moved the soil around the hand with short-handled shovels.

It wasn't long before the discovery of the two bodies was complete. They found an older man who clearly had been hit in the head with a sharp item, most likely a hatchet or tomahawk. He had burns across his head and upper body. The dead woman may have been killed by other means. The smell and status of decomposition made for a difficult onsite assessment of how she may have died. There was no conversation between the men. It was a quiet and somber excavation. Zadock mumbled a little while he took notes in a black field book. The discovery of bodies on this trail was not something to take lightly. The violent method of their death unsettled the men, as all of the people of Kanab knew this trail well and did not want lingering trouble from unruly white folks. It was clear this was not an Indian attack due to the burying of the dead.

The next day, Zadock sat in his home study back in Kanab. He contemplated all the people he had encountered as travelers and was reminded by his recollection of the peculiar nature of the black man, the cowboy, and the young girl. This group was out of the ordinary and seemed the logical first suspects. It was such an unusual occurrence to have this blend of travelers come through Kanab. Zadock counted back the days on his calendar and compared his findings to the decomposition of the bodies. It seemed reasonable and even likely that this was connected. He made note of these travelers and his assumptions in his telegraph to Sheriff Mulvenon of Yavapai County, Arizona Territory.

The bodies were buried on October 21, 1886, in the North Kanab Cemetery. Kanab was a newer town that had recently been growing, so there were not many deaths and the cemetery held only a handful graves. Only stones were placed to locate the Clevengers' graves. Zadock had not yet learned of their identities, but would work to properly mark the graves of the unknown bodies if and when he was successful.

~~~~~~~~~~ *Chapter 15* ~~~~~~~~~~

A Sheriff's Hunt
October 31, 1886

The spurs rang as the short posse man stomped in with long strides to the Yavapai County sheriff's office. While loosening the dirty brown neckerchief around his throat, he dusted off his long-sleeved cotton shirt. He was holding a piece of paper, a telegram card.

The posse man spoke loudly to the sheriff. "Sheriff, ever since Tewksburys started this running sheep business all hell seems to have broken loose. Sometimes I think they brought in the sheep last year just to spite the Grahams. No cattleman in this state knows what to do. Accusations of rustling are way out of hand and it's going to get worse if this keeps up."

.. Although a small man, his stature and presence was felt. His wide chaps and Merwin and Hulbert 1st model Army pistol was holstered on his left side for a cross grab. He wore a neck bandana and a round, flat-brimmed hat. His cotton shirt was stained down his chest and under his arms nearly to his belt. This deputy of sorts was well equipped and was clearly a seasoned lawman.

The sheriff pinched his long handlebar mustache with his fingers before taking the telegram from the posse man. The sherriff removed his hat. He ran his left hand over his large, round, and nearly bald head with concern, scratching as he took a moment to think. Sheriff Mulvenon addressed the posse man. "Damn those Grahams and Tewksburys. I bet they don't even remember why they are fighting. Four years and no end in sight. Who knows how many more are going to have to die?"

"Here ya go, Sheriff. This just arrived for you. Telegram from a judge named Zadock Judd up in Utah. Looks like Kanab. Something bad went down up there. It's out of the way of this cattle war, so I don't think it has anything to do with this mess we are dealing with."

"Thank you." Sheriff Mulvenon then read the telegram to himself.

"Looks like I'm gonna be heading out of here for a while. Let's discuss this. I'm going to need you to watch after things while I'm out. Couple of folks just north of House Rock were killed and buried in shallow graves. This is the second time I've had to deal with this type of incident in just a short time. I should be spending more time on finding the Barney Martin family murderers, but that trail was cold the day we started with no meaningful details from anyone. I'm thankful Judd has some details and some suspects for this issue. This makes for a worthwhile trip north. The Mormons hold a tight community and will all be talking about these strangers passing."

The posse man nodded in agreement, "Yup. Not like them Francisco Vega banditos we couldn't get to squeal. But that's for another time, Sheriff. I'll keep order while you're out. I 'spect you'll be leaving soon as mornin'?"

"Yes. I have to let my wife know what's happened and will be prompt about leaving."

The sheriff handed down some short administrative orders for the deputy and explained his departure plan.

The route north to Kanab could have been shorter, but the sheriff's intuition was to make for Camp Windy and start with a baseline. This would be where anyone traveling out of Arizona north from the middle or east side of Arizona Territory would have passed through and gathered fresh supplies. A base point to understand more about the suspects seemed appropriate, if in fact they had traveled from this part of the territory.

"Sheriff, didn't 'spect to see you comin' through." J. Swap saw Sheriff Mulvenon watering his two horses just after arriving at Camp Windy. The men shook hands. It was obvious they had met each other on previous occasions.

"Yes. Let's have a bite to eat. I have a few questions for you. I'm investigating another murder. This time I have reason to believe you may have seen the suspects in question."

The Sheriff passed his horse to a stable boy and followed J. Swap to a building with only a few tables. Swap motioned to a lady, who brought some fresh fruit and some biscuits for the men.

"So, J., word has it that there was a group of travelers may have come through here sometime back in mid-April or so. Black fellow and a cowboy with a young girl. You recall?"

"Absolutely, Sheriff. Had an old man and his wife named Clevenger. I remember his name 'cause I know some folks from down Safford way that talked about the Clevenger family. That old man apparently set up quite a drainage program with a reservoir of sorts and some tributaries. Smart fella, I recon. Did quite well down there with land and water dealin'. His wife wasn't well. She was sick and the travelin' didn't seem agreeable. You reckon he killed someone?" Swap looked at Mulvenon with curiosity.

Mulvenon adjusted his vest and replied, "Nope. I believe you just gave me the victim's identification. I only know of the Negro, the cowboy, and the girl. These three passed through Kanab a while back, but there were no others with them. The victims were an old woman and an old man, buried in shallow graves just at the top of the Buckskin Mountain grade, at the first campsite. I received a telegram from Zadock Judd in Kanab of the incident and some of these details about the travelers."

Swap scratched his chin. "Well, I'll be. You know that Clevenger feller wasn't the approachable type. He walked around barkin' orders like he had a claim on that little girl and that Negr-uh too. I remember 'cause we tried our best to keep out of that old man's business. We kept quiet and didn't cause a scene, even though we maybe should have. That old man was a real pain, but that group wasn't near as unsettling as them Injuns. Since the Cavalry finally ran down Geronimo we been relieved. But that's all happened since then. Navajo, Apache, Hopi…they seem to be leaving us white folks alone for the time being and keepin' to themselves as of late. No word of any raids recently from passersby or our fort scouts."

Mulvenon shook Swap's hand and led his horse off to be stabled

The sheriff stayed the night and departed just before sunrise. Mulvenon was a persistent man and did not waste time. He estimated his trip to come in around $500, but after Camp Windy he knew he would fall short due to the high price of the dried fruit, beans, and jerky. The effects of the cattle war and the Indian raids made for expensive sundries and dried foods.

Chapter 16

Reckoning

"I'm only half Negro," John said with a friendly tone and a half smile to a table of miners. "Part of me is white. Maybe you jist let the other part be, I'd be mighty obliged. I've got some money so just deal me in and never mind my colored half. I'll keep him in the corner and quiet."

One of the older miners spoke up. "Just let him sit down. We can send him packin' after we take his money. 'Sides, I ain't seen a Negro since 'fore the war. He ain't no harm. Look there, he ain't even got a pistol in that holster. Who in hell walks around with a Cavalry belt and no gun in the skin?"

John pulled a chair from a vacant table and sat. He didn't allow an explanation of his missing sidearm. His decision to make for Nevada was based on the rumors of Goldfield, Nevada's successful mines. He planned to try his hand at solo mining, but not too close to large populations. The cash he and Frank split from the stock sales was enough to purchase some supplies to start his new life mining. John made his way alone from Toquerville northwest to Duckwater, Nevada. He longed for a remote, less occupied town to keep his head low. Duckwater seemed to be an excellent fit.

"Say there, son, where you from? It be a might bit unusual to see any nigrus out this way. You sure you ain't lost?"

"No, sir. I just looking to find some place to settle down some and maybe start my own claim." John purposely answered the old miner with little detail.

"Up north at the border is a new reservation, boys. But do you know what that means for us down here?"

A young miner at the table replied, "Means' the Injun war round here is over and them Injuns can have some of their own land up there."

The old miner laughed aloud with a cough that sounded as if his lungs were full of gravel. "Ha, ha! You dumb sum-bitch! Cavalry finally let them Paiutes and Shoshone have a place all right, but this is all new to them and I aim to scoot further south quick. You never know what day them li'l Injuns decide they all grown up and gonna avenge their daddies. I aim to skip a nighttime throat slittin' and find a safe hole to mine somewhere's else. Soon as all the Cavalry rides out, I won't be far behind 'em. Pissed-off Injuns are unpredictable. War may be over, but that don't mean them gut eaters don't have a bone to pick. As long as somes been left alive, somes gonna be sideways, and that will last forever, no matter what. Mammas, babies, brothers, it don't matter. They all's gonna have a bone to pick. No different than you n' I. We all would do the same thing. It just may be us pickin' bones with those that wronged us and whatnot."

"There any hostiles round here to be worried 'bout?" John asked timidly.

"Not so much as of late," the old miner replied, then spat into a brass spittoon.

John left the table without much to say. He picked up his supplies, loaded a horse and a mule with some essential supplies, and rode northwest to survey the range for his claim.

Setting up camp against some cobbled rocks stopped the wind from snuffing John's fire. He dipped his head and slept.

Throughout the next several weeks, John dug. He dug with fury and disgust. His knowledge of mining was near nothing. He had no mentor and no experience. Word of mouth and conversations on mineral identification were all he had to reference. He started his first attempt chipping and digging where a white quartz vein diagonally crossed a rock slope. The old miners talked about how gold formations sometimes mixed within the quartz layers and could spider into the white. This seemed to fit the bill. John continued to work, and with the weather holding up nicely, he slept outside near a juniper tree and some wind-breaking boulders with nothing more than a small fire in the evenings and early morning.

This morning would prove to be quite unsettling.

Thump.

John's deep rest was interrupted by something nudging his boot.

Thump thump. There it was again.

"Hey there."

A deep voice broke the early morning silence. John rolled to his side and looked up through squinted eyes.

"Yeah, I'm awake. What can I help you…"

John stopped speaking when his eyes cleared and focused on the end of Sheriff Mulvenon's rifle barrel.

"Move slow, boy."

The sheriff motioned with his Winchester. "Keep them hands where I can see 'em."

John slowly stood up and kept his eyes on the end of the rifle doing exactly as told. The sheriff took John's hands and clamped the steel cuffs tightly.

"This is my claim, Sheriff. I rambled around some and lern't this here spot ain't nobody's claim." John spoke with uncertainty to whom he was addressing.

"Boy, tell me about an old man and a lady down in Arizona."

"Uh…no sir, I believe I ain't got nothin' to say 'bout that."

"Suit yourself. It's a long ride back to Arizona Territory. I reckon you know why I'm here anyhow."

The sheriff saddled John's mare and helped him mount up. He then unlatched one rein and used it as a lead rope. They rode south, leaving John's makeshift campsite and his random belongings with exception of his bedroll and some clothing. They were headed to Arizona Territory.

"Hey, John!" Frank yelled from across the Prescott Prison yard.

Whap! Mulvenon slapped the butt of his rifle against the side of Frank's head. "Shut up and turn around." The sheriff had just returned from a law enforcement collaborative effort, collecting Frank and Jessie from Idaho. His temperament was short, to say the least. "You boys will have plenty of time to reminisce. I don't wanna hear you say nuthin fer now." Jessie was being held separately in an office for questioning. Mulvenon removed the cuffs from Frank's skinny wrists and led the prisoners inside. He kicked him into a cell and slammed the flat iron grid door. Frank was now the freshest inmate in the Prescott Prison.

Frank barked at Mulvenon just as he locked the cell door and started to walk away. "Surprised you put us in the same cell, sheriff!"

The sheriff answered without turning around. "Why you surprised? You the only one can get along with that...that blackie, and we ain't got the space for everyone gittin' they own cell."

Mulvenon went directly to Jessie in the office. The prison guard opened the door after the sheriff pounded twice with his fist.

"Jessie, we don't need you yappin' your jaw 'bout nuthin'. We're keeping you here till them two boys get their trial over with. You can be sure your testimony will be heard by the jury so don't be getting no ideas that you're getting outta here. Nobody really knows what the hell to believe between the three of ya."

"I told you, Sheriff, it was that damn nigger boy who done it. Frank and I just got away as soon..."

"Save it for the jury there, missy. I ain't the one to hear none of this."

Jessie continued with her explanation but Mulvenon interrupted her again. "Just, just stop talking. I listened to your ramblin's for days. I'll let you pass that all to the court. You'll be questioned soon enough. I've done my part."

Jessie sat restless and unsure of the officer taking her statement. This deputy of Yavapai County had small, round glasses with a tiny chain than dangled annoyingly against his cheek. Her nerves were shot, ultra-sensitive to even the wood chair arms that seemed cool and hard. A fly landed on the back of her hand, and the tiny legs seemed to be needle sharp. The deputy was on the opposite side of comfort. He sniffed and dug feverishly in his nose. He looked hot and sweaty and let out several heavy breaths of relief that he was indoors and sitting down.

"OK, Miss...ummmm, Clevenger. Jessie Clevenger. Is this your full name?"

"Yes, sir." Jessie sat vertical and stiff.

"This is routine for the court. We already have the statements from Mr. Frank Willson and Mr. John Johnson as to how this whole incident transpired. Your statement is simply for the record of the court." The deputy lied. Frank and John had agreed to never speak of this incident. It was discussed as far back as Navajo Wells that each would place blame on one another if either man spoke even a word. The statement Frank and John each gave to this same deputy was simply, "I don't know nothin' 'bout nothin'."

The deputy continued, "Miss Clevenger, I will write your statement as we talk, so bear with me. I am good at writing, but you may be faster than my pen. You sure are a looker, Miss Clevenger. We don't see many women in these walls from day to day, and surely not one of your caliber. I appreciate your cooperation in this matter. Would you like something to drink?"

"No, sir. Thank you." Jessie didn't realize that the deputy's attempt to appeal to her good nature was not for her benefit.

"Let's begin."

The deputy inked the last few notes and thanked Jessie for all she had done to make this an expedited hearing. He yelled aloud for a guard outside and for him to escort her out for a hot meal.

Frank and John were told a few days prior by the evening guard that a jury had been selected and a court date was set. Today was that day, and the two men still did not know what information, if any, had been disclosed regarding the fate of Samuel and Charlotte.

Frank was nervous of what Jessie might say. Jessie was young and naïve. Frank and Jessie were together. Jessie's hate for John seemed to make Frank's presence draw Jessie physically close to him when the three were within proximity of one another. Frank had spoken fondly of John throughout the time after the group split. John never disrespected Frank, and Frank held John in high regard to this fact. Jessie just seemed to fundamentally hate John because of her upbringing, disliking Negroes simply because they were Negroes. Samuel was not a Confederate by nature of the war—he was from the North, a Yankee—but that did not make him a fan of the concept and reality of freed slaves. There was a minority of the North that sided with the Confederates, and Samuel was of this sort.

Jessie's attachment to Frank was strong, but complicated. Frank was Jessie's first. Her first everything. But the sensible side of her knew she should let him go because of the trouble that was clearly ahead. She chose to linger in Prescott and spent little time away from the prison, hoping that Frank would somehow squeeze out of this debacle. Though she knew it was inevitable that she'd have to move on eventually, her heart was absolute in staying as long as possible. Frank knew this. He also knew she would most likely place blame on John. Frank was not naïve, and knew if the court was what he knew of typical court systems, they would pull the truth out of her young, fragile mind without much resistance. This was not up for discussion between Frank and John. Frank thought about this constantly and knew John worried about Jessie and what she might say. John feared Jessie controlled his fate and it would be Jessie who sent him to the noose.

June 14, 1887, was here. It was a Tuesday. The jury sat quietly in their seats watching the escorted prisoners make their way to their seats. The simplicity of the standard proceedings went quickly. John and Frank were respectable throughout these introductory motions. Frank and John's attorney was L. W. Eggers. He was quiet. Very quiet. His review of the case left little to desire. The prosecution had an eyewitness, and his clients had nothing of use in way of a bargaining chip. A guilty murder conviction followed by the death penalty seemed most likely.

Jessie took the stand. She was sworn in and sat down. The prosecutor, Attorney General Herndon, asked Jessie in a calm voice, "Miss Clevenger, please give the court and jury a detailed description of the incident as you recall. No need to rush. Take your time, and try to remember each detail. Although we have your statement, I would like you to give the court your firsthand account. If it helps, just close your eyes, or focus downward or on me, as if you are only telling me of the incident for the first time."

Jessie fidgeted. She worked very hard to not make eye contact with Frank or John. Taking Herndon's advice, she began.

"We were all in camp."

"A bit louder, Miss Clevenger. If you would, please."

"Sorry, sir. We were all in camp that morning. I was just about to put some coffee on the fire when I heard Frank say to my papa..."

Herndon interrupted. "Your papa, Mr. Samuel Clevenger, correct?"

"Yes, sir. Samuel. Frank said that Samuel had lived long enough and called him a son of a bitch. Frank had an ax and he stuck it right in my papa's head. I started to run and when I got in the trees I stopped and looked back. John the nigger boy was dragging papa out of the fire and by our tent. He dropped papa and ran into the tent. That's when Mama called out for me. So I started to run back and then the gun went off. Mama was moanin' and gurgled and then I stopped. She went quiet and John came out around the tent. He saw me standing there, but he didn't do nuthin'. Later on them two split up the money that they found in Papa's clothes. That's what happened."

"Thank you, Jessie. That will be all from me for now, Judge." Herndon returned to his chair.

Eggers stood for his cross examination and asked Jessie, "Miss Clevenger, were you intimate with my client, Frank Willson?"

"After they killed my folks, Frank and I got close. But I was scared and I did it because he made me."

Frank slammed the table and caught her attention. He pointed at her and yelled out, "Jessie, damn it! What are you..."

The judge slammed his gavel. "Order, boy! Another outburst like that and I'll have you thrown in the Snake Den down in Yuma!" The Snake Den was a dark cave carved into a caliche hill that every prisoner in the Yuma Territorial Prison feared. This dark hole had no light and was simply a locked-up dirt hole. It was the most primitive solitary confinement in use.

Frank sat back and stared sad and disgusted at Jessie. Eggers continued with more meaningless character questions to try for a futile character flaw scenario, but he had nothing that could sway a jury after what they had just heard. Eyewitness testimony is gold for the prosecution.

The *Arizona Champion* weekly newspaper reported that the jury had taken only forty minutes to deliberate. The *Clifton Clarion* reported it had taken only twenty minutes for the jury to deliberate and convict the two men of first-degree murder.

Frank and John were emotionless when the verdict was read aloud. They were escorted quickly back to their cell to await their judgment day.

"Rekonin', Frank, and you n' me we is on the wrong side of this rekonin'. I thought that little Jessie really liked you, but she sure put an end to us fellas. Forgot about all that hate she had for them Clevengers."

"Yup. Now me and you are gonna swing." Frank spoke no more of the incident to John, and John had no more to say today.

The judge sat in his chambers after the trial. He wrote the final statement as the court—and as he—understood this incident and its final verdict for the record.

In his hand he wrote:

This (Yavapai), County –
That in the 19th day of May 1886 they reached a point called House Rock in said County of Yavapai, in the Buckskin Mountains – That they remained in camp through that day + night – That in the morning of the 20th of May, 1886 they left House Rock and started in towards Navajo Wells the next watering place of importance just across the Utah line –
That they did not reach Navajo Wells that night, but camped about 4 o'clock in the afternoon of said 20th day of May, near the top of the Buckskin Mountains and about 7 miles south of the Utah line in this County.
That they remained in camp until next morning, when Johnston + Wilson got up + made a fire, then Mr. Clevenger got up + Jessie began preparing for breakfast –
That Mr. Clevenger sat down in front of the fire, being but partially dressed –
That Mrs. Clevenger being in feeble health was still in bed, in the tent which they had with them + in which all the parties slept at night but Johnston + Wilson.

That as Mr. Clevenger was sitting by the fire said Johnston went + picked up an axe sitting by the side of tree + walked up to Mr. Clevenger + raising the ax, said you have lived long enough you damned old son of a bitch, + stuck Clevenger in the head, killing him instantly knocking him in the fire – that Wilson was standing nearby – that Johnston then caught Clevenger by the clothing + dragged him out of the fire – then Wilson ran to the tent – that after a moment or so, the girl Jessie who had ran away when Clevenger was struck, heard Mrs. Clevenger call his name + then heard her groan –

That in a short while the girl Jessie saw Johnston + Wilson carrying fire up to same cedar trees nearby + failed to make a fire.

That Wilson then went to the girl Jessie (who was about 15 years of age) + told her to come + get in the wagon they were ready to go – that Wilson threatened her + told her to keep her mouth shut – that in the night Wilson slept with the girl Jessie Clevenger, and continued to sleep with her until arrested –

That the next day in the same day of the killing of Samuel Clevenger, that said Johnston, Wilson took the wagon, horses + entire outfit + started on the road with the girl Jessie Clevenger – reaching Kanab Utah that day, when they were recognized by parties who had seen them + talked with them at House Rock in the road after leaving them the day previous –

That Wilson was asked where the "Boss" was + made no reply – That on the night after the murder Wilson gave to Johnston $220 in money – that Samuel Clevenger had about $450 or $500 at the time he was killed – That afterward Johnston + Wilson divided the stock + outfit between –

That in the month of October 1886 the dead bodies of Samuel + Charlotte Clevenger were discovered buried in one hole in the ground near the top of Buckskin Mountains – That the body of Clevenger was partially dressed – + that there were two wounds upon the head which appeared to have been made with an ax –

That the body of Charlotte was dressed in her night clothes – that she had a wound on the head as if made with the back of an ax – the bodies were buried near the surface + the coyotes or some animals had partially mutilated the bodies –

That the bodies were laid one on top of the other – the head of the man towards the north + of the woman towards the south –

That on the grave there had been built a fire – That near the grave were stakes to which tent sides had been fastened – pieces of rope still fastened thereto, which had been cut – a camp fire in the remains of what was nearby – in which was found buttons, pieces of clothing, spectacles, etc. and on the body of Samuel Clevenger, in his pants pocket were found his knife, his toothpicks –

The defendant Johnston was arrested in the month of January east in the state of Nevada + Wilson soon after in Idaho Territory, and after indictment they were tried + convicted of murder of the first degree the jury affixing to their verdict the death penalty.

I have the honor to be

Most respectfully,

James N. Wright,

Prescott, District Judge

June 30th, 1887

Chapter 17

August 7, 1887
Prescott, Arizona Territory Prison

"John. I been thinkin'. I don't mean just regular like, but I been really thinkin' 'bout an idea that might get one of us outta here alive."

John sat up from his bunk and stood up. He walked to the bars of the cell front and looked out. "Well, spit it out. I don't rightly think you have that kind of smarts, but I got nothing to do but hear you out."

"Well, the way I see it, each of us, we never said nothin' to nobody 'bout what happened besides what Jessie spilled. And I figure it just ain't right that both of us gotta swing for this. If you'n me play some cards, poker, seven up, whatever, maybe the loser can confess that he did the killin' alone. Write it all down. Ya know, just tell it how it was only one man's doin'. I bet that judge and sheriff may think about their own morality and judgement day if one of us made a statement like 'at. If'n they's God-fearin' folks, maybe they'd let one of us live. Probably be stuck here for life, but alive. Swingin' an innocent man isn't in their best interest if their Jesus gots anything to say about it…. I just bet they wouldn't take that chance."

John smiled and huffed his breath. "Damn it, Frank. I do believe that's the damnedest idea I ever heard. I'm ready for this. I'll tell you somethin' else. Betcha them sum-bitches will write stories and maybe even a real book about us if it works. I like seven up, but poker is a gentleman's game."

Frank answered quickly. "I ain't no gentleman, so let's do seven up. Seven's supposed to be a lucky number. I guess maybe we will put that to the real test."

The card game was on. The night sweats, restless hours of anticipation, and uncertainty of this moment gave both men the appearance of prisoners locked up for decades and not just several months.

Frank placed the remaining cards stacked perfectly between them. John and Frank both had their seven cards fanned perfectly and symmetrically. Each man spent every extra second to make sure each card was in its rightful place, as if it made the dealt hands something better. The smell of John's vomit seemed to get stronger as the minutes rolled by. Frank was disappointed to see his cards, but kept his composure. John had some residual sweat mixed with tears running down his face. His red eyes and sickly pale skin didn't give up his quality starting hand.

Each player made sure his choices were surely thought out to the fullest, as each man's neck was literally on the line. Soon, the game came to an end. Frank wiped his face with both hands, and with an added ironic chuckle he said to John, "Ha! Well, son, I will pray for you…for as long as I have left in this damned ol' place. Guard! Hey, guard, get me that court officer—the one who wrote down our statements…or someone who matters. I gotta story that needs some fixin'."

The guard nodded, spit some tobacco into a brass spittoon, and stood from his chair. He dropped the hangman's noose on the floor next to another completed noose he had finished tying earlier. Only a few minutes later he returned with the Yavapai County deputy wearing the same small glasses and dangling chain. The deputy spoke to John and Frank directly. "I will provide you with this paper and pen. Whatever you write will not make much difference in the coming day or two. I s'pose you have some kin to write to, so get after it. I'll be back in an hour or so and take what you have."

Frank sat down and began to write. Just as John and he described this would be written, Frank penned the words and spoke them aloud as he continued. Word for word, and in Frank Wilson's hand, this is what he wrote:

Prescott August 9th, 1887

This is to certify that John A Johnson is innocent of the crime of which he stands convicted on the 20th day of May 1886 the day on which Samual Clevinger was killed Johnson left the camp earley in the morning to hunt some horses that had strayed of during the night with orders to drive them on to water as soon as he found them as there was no water where we were camped and after Johnson had been gone from camp about one hour I Frank Willson became engaged in a quarrel with Samual Clevenger and his wife Charlotte Clevenger and killed them both and buried them in the same spot where their bodeys were found and then I took the wagon and the rest of the stock and overtook Johnson on the road with the rest of the horses and I told Johnson that Clevenger and his wife had gone to Utah on another road with some friends that cought up with us that morning as there was a road turned of that went into Utah he believed me until we got to Tokerville Utah were I traded of some of the horses and then Johnson asked me what Clevenger would say if he knew that I was tradeing of his horses I told Johnson that I had killed them and he had beter keep still about it for I would say that he helped to kill them or that he killed them both and I made Johnson take some of the horses and some money so he would not say anything about it I am ready to meet my fate but I do not want to see an innocent man hang for my crime

Frank Willson

Prescot August 9th 1896

This is to certify that John A
Johnson is inocent of the crime of
which he stands convicted on the
20th day of may 1886 the day on which
Samuel Clevenger was killed
Johnson left the camp early in
the morning to hunt some horses
that had strayed of dureing the
night with orders to drive them on
to water as soon as he found them
as there was no water where we were
camped and after Johnson had been
gone from camp about one hour I
Frank Willson became engaged in
a quarel with Samual Clevenger and
his wife Charlotte Clevenger and
killed them both and buried them
in the same spot where their bodys
were found and then I took the wagon
and the rest of the stock and overtook
Johnson on the road with the rest of the
horses and I told Johnson that
Clevenger and his wife had gone to
Utah by another road with some
friends that caught up with us that
morning as there was a road turned
of that went into Utah he believed
me untill we got to Tokerville Utah
where I traded of some of the horses
and then Johnson asked me
what Clevenger would say if he
knew that I was trading of his horses

I told Johnson that I had killed
them and he had better keep still
about it for I would say that he
helped to kill them or that he
killed them both and I made
Johnson take some of the horses and
some money so he would not
say anything about it I am ready
to meet my fate but I do not
want to see an inocent man
hang for my crime

Frank Willson

*Frank Willson's actual confession letter. Copyright use granted
by the Archives of the State Library of Arizona.*

Jessie was allowed to talk with Frank through his cell door, in the presence of Sheriff Mulvenon. "Frank, you know this ain't true," she told him. "You know that I saw John draggin' Sam out of that fire and he killed Charlotte right after. What you wrote is wrong, Frank, and you will be damned to hell for sayin' that." The sheriff listened intently while Jessie scolded Frank. John just looked down to his feet and sat on his bunk. He did not acknowledge anything Jessie had to say.

"Sheriff said you wrote nothin' of the sort on how it really happened," Jessie said. "I'm ashamed, and that Negro can go straight to hell with you."

Frank looked at Jessie with sunken eyes. He reached through the square flat iron cell door and brushed his two thumbs lightly across her eyebrows. Jessie's eyes filled with tears that poured down her cheeks. Her heart was racing with confused emotions. She was so mad at Frank but couldn't hold back the pain of what lay ahead for his broken soul. Frank blinked several times before a tear could break and told Jessie, "You look good, girl. You'll be all right. It looks like they been feedin' you good too. Why you here? Are you really mad or are you here 'cause you wanna see me one last time?"

"Frank, I'm here to tell you I got a baby on the way. I don't want it growin' up knowing its daddy has gone to hell for lyin'."

Frank's knees buckled as he processed this news. He drug his hands down the iron cell door as he sat crumpled on his legs and coughed some words when his tears finally broke free. "Ah, damn it. Damn, Jessie. This sure is sumpthin', ain't it? Look what I done to ya. I'm 'shamed at what I done, Jessie, and I aim to have a talk 'bout all this with that Peter fella ifn' I get the chance, or maybe all that's just empty hope too. Either way it don't matter much now. You keep that baby safe, you find yourself a respectable young man to take care of ya. You do it now. No buts 'bout it!"

Frank's eyes burned as he continued. "Tell that baby his daddy was from Michigan. Tell'm he used the name Frank Willson 'cause he been doing things he ain't proud of for a long time and that his real name wasn't for anyone to know. It was a better name for when he was a better person. There was a time when Frank Willson was a better one. This hangin' is for Frank Willson and not for the good man lost inside, or somewheres on a trail. The good man is lost and this carcass of a hell-bound soul ain't much use anyway."

"You know, Frank, they will remember this in a hundred years. Never would a nigger boy be the one to get off so lightly. Never would a self-respectin' white man do what you did for a damn ol' blackie like John."

The sheriff took Jessie by the shoulder and guided her out of the cell block. She turned back with one last look. The sheriff turned Jessie over to a deputy, who took her out of the prison. Mulvenon returned to the cell block and asked the men, "You boys got any other family need notifyin'? I can send a telegram each ifn' you like."

John hopped down from his bunk. "Sheriff, I got a wife n' family in Baltimore. I was born in Trenton, New Jersey. Can I give you the address so as you can tell them my where'bouts?"

The sheriff obliged John's request and took down the information.

Chapter 18

August 11, 1887
Shave & uh Haircut

Frank and John stared into the back cell wall side by side as the town barber cut their hair and shaved their ragged faces. Neither man knew if the confession Frank wrote would be worth the paper it was written upon due to the testimony that actually solidified their conviction. Time was running short; the scheduled execution date was the next day.

"Hey, you miserable bastards," the guard said. "I'm supposed to ask you what denomination ya'll is. Ya know, ifn' want a preacher to come stay wichya."

"Nope. Don't need no preacher man grinding it in for me. John, you?"

"I'd like to see that Catholic priest again. Gobratosi I reckon is his name."

The guard laughed aloud. "Yup, they always get religious a day or two before. The last fella found his God real late. They was ready to put the rope on his neck when he asked for the preacher to give him last rites."

Frank was irritated with the guard's demeanor. "Hey, are you always a jackass or just when you ain't sleepin'?"

The guard replied without hesitation. "Hey, are you gonna die quick, or choke and quiver for a damn hour? Shut the hell up, dead man."

Frank was stunned speechless by the guard's comeback. That ended the banter, and Frank lost the ability to continue. He and John finished their breakfast, and the process of preparing the convicted men progressed. The guard passed the invitation on, and the priest arrived that day. John took to the priest and accepted the priest's console for the time allotted before he and Frank were to be bathed and prepared for the execution.

The barber's hands trembled, but not so much that it affected his ability to give a first-class shave. He knew the gravity of the situation, and that his small part in this process was unnervingly important in sending men to meet their maker. No words were spoken. Each man tried on the new suits provided to them by a local tailor. The suits were perfectly fit to each man; the measurements taken a week prior had been done masterfully. John was comfortable. He had dressed with tight neckline military clothes, but this was new to Frank. Frank had never worn a full suit, let alone something so snug-fitting around his neck. He tugged and pulled at the necktie until he stretched some clearance from his throat. The photographer, Erwin Baur, moved and pushed John into position, snapping a photo. He nudged Frank into position and snapped another photo. Erwin was another quick in-and-out of this process. His expeditious departure was indicative of his hesitance of being in the presence of convicted murders.

At 11:15 a.m. a small group of men led by Sheriff Mulvenon entered the prison cell. Governor Zulick was of the group. Mulvenon read the death warrants to Frank and John. At this time the governor handed Mulvenon an envelope to open and read.

The sheriff read the letter to himself, then said, "The court has taken consideration of your confession, Mr. Willson. Mr. Johnson will not be exonerated from involvement with this crime due to the uncooperative nature of the sworn statements prior to trial. However, Mr. Johnson will be granted a reprieve of sentencing until September 23rd."

"What? What does that mean?" John blared out, uncertain and confused by the sheriff's legal lingo.

"Means you will not hang today, Mr. Johnson. Your sentencing has been suspended until September 23rd by the governor and judge. There is a hearing to determine if life imprisonment is a more suitable punishment in light of Mr. Willson's confession." John's legs instantly collapsed. He fell into the corner of the room, sobbing and choking on his tears. Frank simply stood, nodding with an affirmative yes gesture. He adjusted and pulled the sleeves of his suit with perfect posture.

"August 12, 1887," the sheriff said. "The time has come, Mr. Willson. Please prepare yourself as we approach the stairs. Be strong, son. Keep your legs about you."

Sheriff Mulvenon and a deputy named Hickey marched Frank to the yard.

"Yes, sir, I can get up there." Frank was calm. The moment had become serene. The fear of this day had grown stale over the months since the jury's conviction. The last two days revived the terror, but at this moment it was different.

The three men reached the top of the stairs. A handful of journalists from various newspapers were sent specific invitations to the execution. They were present with pen and paper in hand to report the execution details. The small crowd was quiet and stood twenty or so feet from the gallows, framed high above the ground. Thirteen high steps above the ground. Frank's legs and arms were then pinioned tightly.

"Do you have any final words?" Mulvenon offered.

With a calm smile Frank offered up a quiet, "No, sir." While Frank was still smiling, a second deputy named Tacket approached up the stairs. He placed a black hood over Frank's head and drew the hangman noose down around his neck.

Frank didn't see the black cloth of the hood. He forced his mind back to a conversation about his end and how he wanted it to play out. A clear stream and a large tree. He was nestled in the green grass up to the trunk, watching some ducks pick through some moss. Frank didn't break his concentration and didn't react to Deputy Tacket positioning the knot slightly to the right and cinching.

Mulvenon stepped back near the priest, held his breath, and at exactly twelve minutes past twelve o'clock, he pulled the trap door lever. The floor fell under Frank and the rope whipped tight, snapping Frank's neck instantly. Frank gave only two noticeable twitches with his feet. The sheriff eyed his railroad pocket watch for what seemed to be forever. Doctor Robinson emerged from the crowd and timed Frank's pulse for eighteen minutes as he hung. Robinson always took extra care in verifying that there was nothing of a pulse remaining. He was extremely professional and thorough with this determination of absolute death. After the doctor officially declared Frank dead, Hickey and Tacket lowered Frank's body into a coffin. At 1 p.m. the body was loaded into a wagon and dispersed to the city cemetery.

Jessie had moved on. She had Frank's baby girl and left the birth certificate mostly blank with no mention of Frank Willson as the father. Perhaps not knowing his real name, or for whatever reason, she felt it was best to leave the line blank. She later married a man named Pierce and moved away from the Arizona Territory. There is no documentation of whatever happened to Jessie and her family.

John Johnson's sentence was reduced to life imprisonment. He was sent to the Yuma Territorial Prison. Due to his model prisoner behavior, he was granted release in 1891. Nearly thirty years later a newspaper reported that John had assaulted and threatened the life of his landlord. He was charged with a misdemeanor. His involvement with the Clevenger murder was mentioned in the article. During the interview with the reporter, John divulged the true nature of his release—how he, a mulatto man, had been given his freedom by a white man after a most important game of seven up.

~~~~~~~~~~ *END* ~~~~~~~~~~

March 2003
Utah/Arizona Border

*J*im and Dave were construction workers, both very rugged and in their late forties. Years of working odd construction jobs in Southern Utah easily sours a man's character, and it can encourage a bitter attitude if one's attention is not focused on a particular course of future aspirations. The work environment mixed with drug and alcohol abuse had left them both very aware that they were not on the path to healthy retirement. Jim was the self-proclaimed expert of everything, and Dave was more of the quiet "who cares?" type.

Both men were not really friends per se, but with certain common threads, they were really just stuck with each other. The sparse population of Southern Utah and constant religious tension of non-Mormon residences left the pair very picky about friendships. Theirs was a love-hate relationship. They often blamed their likenesses on society, the environment, Utah, and whatever else sounded good within any random conversation.

After a half-hour drive, Dave finally had enough of Jim's advice on everything from the stock market to how he had told the boss where to stick it. Dave also could see that Jim was lost due to his unsure turns and backtracking out of random, dead-end partial trails. The roads that spider around the top of the Buckskin grade get a little confusing south of Eagle Sink, or as some call it "Wildcat Sink." This was a whole different argument between Jim and Dave for another time. The thick junipers easily turn explorers around if the sun is shaded with clouds or in a rainstorm. This was the norm, wandering various dirt roads made in the '50s and '60s for cattle and sheep.

The talk was mostly a one-way conversation with Jim leading the subject matter as he saw fit. Jim and Dave had worked a long, six-day week. This particular day was all about getting "the hell out," as they often put it. Arrowhead hunting was on the morning agenda. Dave had let Jim in on his so-called "secret spot" for some top-notch Anasazi artifact hunting. Just about every Northern Arizona or Southern Utah hilltop seemed to be littered with artifacts from the pre-Columbian era to Anasazi, or Desert Archaic timeline.

Overtopping some sagebrush off the shoulder of the sandy dirt road, the men finally came to a stop in Dave's brown, late '70s Chevy pickup. Jim slid out of the passenger side and flipped his Marlboro butt into the brush. "Davey, gimmie a smoke."

Dave passed a fresh cigarette across the front seat of the pickup to Jim. After taking a long swig from his fifth of Jack Daniel's, Dave then jumped from the passenger side and lit himself a fresh cigarette. Each man started off in different directions in order to cover more ground. Jim was tall and lean and could cover some serious real estate with one step. Dave was short and equally skinny, but with all the whiskey, his wobble of a walk didn't carry him nearly as quickly as Jim.

It was early March. Eagle Sink was always a bit cool, but today was an exceptional Sunday afternoon and very pleasant. Both men wandered through the thick juniper trees and sagebrush searching for Anasazi artifacts. Dave headed off to the north of the road, mainly to get far enough as to not hear Jim's annoying whistling. Jim had a habit of whistling tunes stuck in his head from the local country radio station.

"Dammit!" Dave yelled, spooked and nearly stepping on a jackrabbit that was crouched in a small patch of brush.

Jim heard Dave's yell and hollered back, "Davey, you ain't outta smokes, are ya?" Jim had a constant fear of running out of cigarettes.

Dave hollered back, "Naw, just a rabbit." About the time Dave found his footing he peered into an opening between a small grove of juniper trees. It looked to Dave that it could have been an old campsite, with rusted cans and broken glass from an old cowboy, or a fence builder's camp. Dave wasn't too surprised, being that these were quite abundant in the area, but an old trash pile is always worth a good look. Dave noticed remnants of some black dirt and some charred wood—what might have been a fire pit. He then saw what looked to be most of a lantern, rusted and still hanging under a juniper tree, about six feet off the ground. This was a nice find, something he could hang on the porch of his house. It would be a nice accent to the few other rusted farm tools and traps he displayed at his front door. He leaned into the tree and pulled the lantern from the thick limb, snapping a few smaller limbs as the lantern's bail broke free of the juniper.

Dave just started to walk away from the tree when he blurted, "Dammit! Son of a..." He had stubbed his toe and tripped up on a root, or a rock wedged in the stiff sand. "You outta smokes now?" Dave heard the faint yell of Jim again.

"No, I hit my..." Stopping in midsentence, Dave recognized the steel handle of a revolver—with the grips long since deteriorated or missing—standing straight up from the sand.

Colt Single Action Army found loaded with .44-40
and .45 colt cartridges

"Hey, Jimmy, git over here and check this out!" Dave yelled.

No more than two inches were exposed; the rest of the gun was completely buried. It took Dave more than a good tug to release the gun from the stiff gravel and sandy ground. He buffed off the cylinder and barrel with his hand enough to see what it was. Dave wasn't a gun expert by any stretch of the word. He owned an old Winchester .30-30 his dad had given him and an older .30-06 that had seen its better days, but that was it. Though he didn't know the details, the gun Dave pulled from the ground was a Colt Single Action Army with five live rounds still in the cylinder. You could easily read the back of the first cartridge as a .44-40. The other visible cartridge in the cylinder was a .45. The three remaining seemed to match the slug type matching the .45. The gun was rusted with the loading gate open, and seized enough that there were no loose parts. The barrel length was five and one-eighth inches long with a nonstandard, dovetailed front sight. These artillery models originally had a longer barrel, but many opted to have them shortened for reasons like buckboard riding and quicker access. The pistol was far from repairable, but nonetheless a neat find.

Jim soon emerged through the trees, and Dave showed him what he'd found. "Don't think I can fix it, but I can hang it somewhere at the house."

Jim pinched the cigarette out of his mouth and motioned with it. "Hey, you oughta stop by the post office counter. Daniel Swapp's dad, Eldon, out there in Johnson, is always buying and tradin' for dug-ups and old stuff. I bet you could trade him for somethin' more useful. Maybe somethin' that ain't busted even, like a coyote gun or something."

Dave nodded. "Yep, maybe so." He held up the lantern in front of him. "Found this too. It was hangin' right there. Gonna take it home, stick it up on the porch. Elaina might like that."

Jim took his turn and pulled his right front pocket out of his Levi's to show Dave his two arrowheads. The two men started their walk through the brush towards the truck. Jim bummed another cigarette.

While still walking, Dave leaned low, mid stride, and picked up a shard of flint without stopping. It wasn't an arrowhead, as he had first suspected. Walking slowly through the brush and near a juniper tree, he finished rubbing the sand from the smooth shard and flicked it toward the tree. Not looking to where it landed, he continued to the truck. The shard landed under an exposed wire bail under the tree. The wire bail of an iron pot. By now, Dave was running short on cigarettes and Jim's sixth sense knew it.

The two men agreed silently to get back to town. Time to hit Stage Stop for the essential Marlboros and maybe a honey bun to warm on the dash.

The End

CPSIA information can be obtained
at www.ICGtesting.com
Printed in the USA
LVOW07s1520110417
530416LV00005B/1020/P